# THE BEAUTIFUL
# SCREAMING OF PIGS

Damon Galgut was born in Pretoria in 1963 and now lives in Cape Town. He wrote his first novel, *A Sinless Season*, when he was seventeen years old. His other books include *Small Circle of Beings*, *The Quarry* and, in 2003, *The Good Doctor*, which was shortlisted for the Man Booker Prize, the Commonwealth Writers Prize and the International Dublin IMPAC Literary Award.

# THE BEAUTIFUL SCREAMING OF PIGS

## DAMON GALGUT

Atlantic Books
London

First published by Scribners, Great Britain 1991
Published in Abacus by Little, Brown and Company 1992
Revised edition published by Penguin Books (South Africa) (Pty) Ltd 2005

This paperback edition published by Atlantic Books, an imprint of Grove
Atlantic Ltd, in 2006.

1 3 5 7 9 8 6 4 2

A CIP catalogue record for this book is available
from the British Library.

1 84354 462 8

Printed in Great Britain by
Mackays of Chatham plc, Chatham Kent

Atlantic Books
An imprint of Grove Atlantic Ltd
Ormond House
26–27 Boswell Street
London
WC1N 3JZ


www.groveatlantic.co.uk

*For SIA and for NIGEL*

It's not easy to be on this earth
With its warrior stars and furious men;
It's hard to pierce the night
And difficult to see the day;
But if we aren't careful
With every moment, every sight,
The dark will come in with the tide
And the future will wipe us out.

*Ajax* by Sophocles
Translated by Robert Auletta

## Author's Note

This book has troubled me since it was first published in 1991. The rhythms of the language have always sounded discordant on my ear. It has been many years since it was last in print, but now that it is being reissued, I have taken the opportunity to rework it. It is not a new book, but it's not quite the old one either.

A bit of historical background is perhaps in order. At the end of World War I, the German colony of South West Africa was placed under South African mandate. Later, South Africa refused to hand it over to the United Nations, choosing instead to fight a long and bloody war with the South West Africa People's Organisation (SWAPO). In 1989, under the interim control of the United Nations Transition Assistance Group (UNTAG), South West Africa held its first free elections.

# THE BEAUTIFUL
# SCREAMING OF PIGS

# CHAPTER ONE

We came down the drive. The headlights picked out the house, the garage, the silent, patient figure in front.

'Oh yes,' said my mother. 'There she is. Waiting for us. She's always waiting. Like the sphinx.'

'Mom,' I said.

She came forward to welcome us. Diminutive, dour, she was wearing the same soiled apron I remembered from every previous visit. It was two years since I'd last been here.

She came to me first. 'Patrick,' she said. She held me by the shoulders.

'Hello, *Ouma*,' I said.

Then she went to my mother. They embraced cautiously, with tender hostility, in the wash of light from the car. The engine was still running.

I was given the room in the attic, where the roof sloped down. I had always slept here, since I was a small boy, in the days and days I'd stayed on this farm, when my mother still loved my father.

I unpacked my clothes, though it wasn't necessary to do so: we were leaving again the next day. But for some reason the orderly routine, as well as the friction of fingers on cloth, was comforting to me. I sorted and stashed my clothes into drawers and pushed them carefully closed. Then I sat on the bed, staring out the window, to where the last of the sunlight was fading. It gave me a small shock when I turned to see my mother watching me from the doorway, her arms folded across her chest. I didn't know how long she'd been there.

'You gave me a fright,' I told her.

'Sorry. I thought you knew I was here. Do you want a pill?'

'No. Thank you.'

'Supper's almost ready.'

'I'll be there,' I said. 'I'm coming now.'

But she didn't go. She stayed there, watching me.

We sat in the dining room, my grandmother, mother, myself. We ate in silence, our iron spoons dashing the plates, and I kept my gaze fixed downwards, on the surface of the table in front of me. There were burn marks and scratches and stains in the wood, a whole history of damage. A chill was coming up from the slate floor, like the presence of the house added to our own.

*Ouma* sat at the head of the table, in the place she'd occupied ever since her husband had died a couple of years ago. Whenever she needed anything she would lean forward and ring a heavy metal bell with a shake of her wrist; the surprisingly delicate note it gave off summoned a black woman, who came in from the kitchen on bare feet.

'Anna,' my mother said the first time she saw her, 'how are you?'

Anna gave a little curtsy and a shy smile, but she didn't answer. I had no memory of Anna from before, but the servants were moved around from job to job on the farm at my grandmother's whim, so she may have been hidden behind the scenes somewhere. *Ouma* disapproved of friendly connections with her underlings, and frowned almost imperceptibly now through the deep silence that set in the cold room, in which the only audible sound was the scraping of Anna's feet on the floor.

After supper, we moved out to the back stoep. We sat in a row on three wooden chairs, looking out towards the mountains. The moon was up and in its light bats were flying and flickering over the orchard.

'When are you leaving? You don't want to stay an extra day?'

'No, no,' my mother said. 'We have to go in the morning, after breakfast. We have a schedule to keep to.'

'Ah,' *Ouma* said with ironic awe. 'A *schedule*.' She sucked on her teeth and said to me, 'Your father called, Patrick.'

'Howard called here?' my mother said, incredulous.

'He wants you to phone him tonight.'

'Oh, right,' I said. 'Okay. Sure.'

'It's a power trip,' my mother said. 'He's trying to get at me. Don't call him, Patrick.'

Anna came in on her flat, calloused feet, bringing coffee on a tray.

'*Hoe voel jy*, Patrick?' *Ouma* said.

'All right,' I said. 'I'm much better, actually.'

'*Heeltemal gesond*?'

'No,' I said. 'That will take a long time.'

She made a sound in her throat that could have been sympathy or disapproval and slurped her coffee. My

3

mother looked sideways at me and winked.

My mother, though it was hard to believe, had grown up here on the farm. In my younger years my visits here had been filled with wonder at this fact. I had walked about the dusty veld, trying to work out how it had given rise to her. There was no trace of her rural beginnings in my mother's face. No evidence of this other, earlier self in the woman who had brought me up.

There was an old photograph of her – small and sepia – hanging next to the phone and I studied it now as I held the receiver and turned the handle to get the operator. It showed a little girl in a dark dress, standing against a backdrop of trees, her hair in pigtails, grinning for the camera with a square, exact gap where one of her front teeth was missing.

'Hello?'

'Cape Town,' I said and gave the number. There was a sibilant pause before it began to ring. My father's voice was loud. 'Howard,' he said, speaking it like an accusation.

'Dad?'

Another pause. 'Patrick?'

'Yup.'

'How are you?'

'Fine. I'm fine.'

'You taking your medicine?'

'Yup. What's the matter?'

'No, nothing. I wanted to find out how you are, that's all. Do you mind?'

'No.'

'How's your grandmother?'

This said with a slight scoff, which for some reason irritated me.

'She's fine.'

'And your mother?' This was the real reason for the conversation; both of us knew it. Although he and my mother had been divorced for some time now, he still felt anxiety whenever she left town, as though she might never come back.

'She's also fine. We're all fine. Dad, what's the matter?'

'Nothing, I told you. Just checking up. I'm your father, do you mind?'

'No,' I said lightly. Some lies are light.

'What time are you going tomorrow?'

'I don't know. After breakfast, Mom said.'

'Okay. What time do you get up to Windhoek?'

'I don't have a clue. I'll call you from up there, when we arrive.'

'Do that. And you take care of yourself.'

When I'd put the phone down the silence seemed to sizzle in my ear. I went back out to the *stoep*, where my mother and grandmother had drawn together into intimacy, holding hands and whispering. They went quiet as I arrived.

'I'm going to bed,' I told them.

'What did he want? Did he ask about me?'

'No.'

I kissed them both goodnight – my grandmother's face rough and cool, my mother's warm and smooth – and went up to the attic. From the window the moon seemed magnified, swelling toward fullness. I undressed and put out the lamp and rolled into bed. I lay there for a long time, my hands behind my head, listening to the sounds of the house. I heard my mother come up to the room underneath; heard her brush her teeth and mutter to herself as she got ready for bed. Then there was quiet. Perhaps another half hour passed before I realised why I hadn't fallen asleep. So I got up and swallowed my pills. Prothiaden, Valium. In a little while I was sleepy. I rolled on my side.

# CHAPTER TWO

We were going up to Windhoek to visit my mother's lover. She had met him there eighteen months before while she was lecturing at the academy. All I knew about him was that his name was Godfrey and that he was twenty-six years old. Also, of course, that he was black.

I wasn't disturbed by this fact. A numbness had crept into my life, so that no fact could hurt me again. My mother, since she had parted from my father, had given herself to much stranger things than this. Living with her in our little cottage in Cape Town, I had been witness to passions far more curious than men. So when my mother had come back from her stint of teaching in Windhoek with news of her lover, I wasn't alarmed by his colour.

I had spoken to Godfrey many times on the telephone. He phoned her twice a week, late at night. In these calls, strangely, he never acknowledged that I was her son, and I didn't refer to his relationship with her. We never called each other by name, though we were always carefully polite. He had a clear, deep, level voice. He called sometimes after midnight. According to my mother, this was his way of trying to catch her out. 'He's madly jealous,' she said – and she fuelled his jealousy by going out when she was expecting him to call. Or she would make me answer the phone sometimes and pretend that she wasn't there.

'I want to talk to Ellen.'

'I'm sorry, but she's out.'

'Out where?'

'I don't know. I'm not sure. With friends.'

'When is she getting back?'

'I really don't know.'

'Tell her Godfrey called. *Godfrey*. Be sure to give her the message.'

'I'll tell her.'

Afterwards she made me describe his tone, and repeat in exact detail what he had said. Although I was happy to play this game for her, I did feel sorry for him, this young man so very much in love. She was seventeen years older than him, and of course I wasn't much younger than he was. She'd got married to my father when she was only twenty. She was still studying drama then, and he had just completed his degree in business science. They were an unlikely match, but my mother had fallen pregnant and one thing led to another. She dropped out of drama school at the end of the year and became a wife.

Although she did try her hand at a few acting jobs over the years, she had never really had a career of her own. Her big role was the one she played as a housewife, a mother, a maker of homes. She set about remoulding herself in the image my father desired. He was ashamed of her rustic Afrikaans beginnings, so she learned to speak English without an accent. She made it her duty to acquire cosmopolitan tastes and values, which she picked up from the people and homes that were the new backdrop to her social life. 'I grew up in a hurry,' she told me bitterly. In exchange, my father provided money and material consolations. We were raised in great style. I arrived in the world three years after my brother Malcolm. By then there was already no trace of that earlier, other woman: Elsa de Bruin had disappeared and in her place there was Ellen Winter, who might have been born in Constantia.

In those years she didn't smile much. I remember a composed, vacant, bloodless face, eyes wide and dark, with long lashes. And her hard mouth, with lips that were slightly too thin to be sensual. It could have been a cruel face, but there was no cruelty in her. Not even the deep grief she later claimed to be feeling – grief for her lost other life – showed up anywhere. Her moods were as level and blank as her face. She was very quiet. I would often come into the lounge, my father and brother out for the evening, to find her sitting alone in a chair, listening to the ticking of clocks which filled the house like a kind of music.

'What are you doing?' I would say, disturbed at this vision of solitary waiting.

'I'm sitting,' she would answer. 'Just sitting.'

I looked for tears, but her face was always passive. Nevertheless, on some level below words, I could sense her pain. I would run at her, butting her with my head, trying to jostle her out of her frozen reverie. Sometimes I succeeded: she might get up with a faint smile and say, 'Go and bath. We're going out for dinner tonight.' Then I would go and get myself ready and meet her downstairs half an hour later, both of us dressed up, as if involved in some old-fashioned courtship. And this strange, chaste illusion would continue through the evening: in half an hour we would be seated opposite each other at an intimate table, while waiters pressed menus into our hands, and a piano played softly in the background.

At times like these I was happy to be alone with my mother, brother and father elsewhere, all rivals for her affection removed. I believed I could make up for the lacks and absences in her life. I would whisper my wishes across the white table-top, the candle flame bending to my breath. 'Let's go for ice cream,' I'd say, 'when we're finished here.'

'All right,' she'd whisper, dropping her voice in thrilling collaboration with my fantasy, 'a big white ice cream, on a cone.'

'And a movie after that.'

'Yes, a movie,' she'd say, falling into a contemplation that only just included me. Movies and ice cream were things that never occurred to my father; I suggested them for exactly that reason. And we walked along the beachfront together, arm in arm, licking our ice creams in a kind of dazed complicity. My mother was white and long and cold, like any ice cream cone.

When I was much younger she allowed me to sleep in her bed sometimes. These were extraordinary nights: half-waking, half-sleeping, I was stranded, it felt, in an acre of sheets. She lay at my side, elegant even in sleep, one arm stretched out next to her. She would let down her hair before she went to bed and it lay strewn across the pillow: a pattern in black, one of the shadows that the moon cast in through the window.

Once – only once – did she cry out in her sleep. A long

and tangled moan that came out in pain: 'Howard... Howie... what have you... *done... ?*'

The meaning of this remained unsolved; a secret buried beneath her white, moonlit face. She breathed softly as she slept. Too softly sometimes: I woke once in the night and thought that she had died. I called and clutched at her with greasy hands, and cried when she woke up and cradled me in her embrace. 'Were you afraid I'd left you... ?' I didn't answer. I couldn't find words to express what it would feel like to be alone in the house with Malcolm, and with Dad.

As I grew older she wouldn't let me share the bed anymore. 'You're too big now,' she said. 'You're not afraid of the dark anymore.' It was never the dark that had driven me to her, but I didn't say anything. In any event, she no longer shared a bed with my father and her new one, in the spare room downstairs, was too small by half. So I stayed in my own room above, emptiness all around, sensing her heat.

When my father was at home all trace of her affection went underground. She became formal and even polite with me. She would sit in the study at night, in one of the leather armchairs, keeping her hands busy with tapestry or sewing or writing a letter. She murmured very softly when she spoke. Only by tiny signs – the brushing of fingers at the table, or a glance toward me in front of the television – was I assured of her continuing love for me, expressed so wholly when we were both alone.

When I remember these scenes now it is a kind of emptiness I feel; and yet our lives were full. Full in the material sense, with objects and ornaments and opportunities for diversion. I had my own room, with a bathroom to myself. Our house was three stories tall, carpeted throughout, the walls covered in expensive paintings, every table laden with china or silver, all of it real. My father, that cultured boor, knew what to buy, though he took no pleasure in it; he was sending out coded signals of wealth and gentility. 'I would rather go to India for the real thing,' he told us, 'than buy a perfect copy in South Africa.' His possessions shored up his precarious high standing.

He needed to advertise his sophistication, because it was entirely fake. His real love was for hunting. The walls downstairs were covered in animal heads. He had killed every one of them, he would tell his visitors proudly, as he showed his collection of guns and rifles. He never tired of handling them, taking them apart and cleaning them, his hands more loving on those hard bits of metal than they'd ever been on us. 'With this,' he would tell you, 'I killed that,' pointing to the head of a kudu above the fireplace. 'And with this one, I took that.' An impala near the door. 'This little baby brought that one down.' A warthog, its bristles shining.

His proudest claim of all was the leopard in the entrance hall. Preserved in its entirety on an island of wood, teeth drawn back in a snarl.

As a boy I was horrified and fascinated by the leopard. I would lie for hours on the cool tiles of the floor, trying to look down its throat into the darkness it contained. I imagined my father, down on one knee, holding steady while the leopard charged. It was a huge disappointment to learn later – from Malcolm, who had been there – that this wasn't the way it had happened at all. 'We chased it for miles in the Land Rover,' he said. 'It was wounded, it couldn't run properly. Dad shot it in a tree when it tried to get away. He didn't even get out.'

My father, for all his ornaments and paintings, looked as if he belonged outdoors. He was a fat and sweaty man, with brown hair cropped short and a neat moustache, stained at the edge with nicotine. He had a heart problem, but he liked to smoke cigars and drink. He had blue eyes so pale as to be almost without colour. He would stare at me sometimes, with amazement or disapproval, from those eyes, rimmed with resin and short white hairs, like the bristles of the warthog on the wall.

'Why are you so small?' he demanded.

'I don't know.'

'You must eat properly. Do you eat?'

'Yes.'

'Ellen, does he eat?'

'Yes, Howie, what are you talking about? You've seen him eating.'

'Do you play sport, Patrick? At school?'

'He doesn't like sports, Howie, you know that.'

'Nonsense,' he bellowed, surging up suddenly onto his short and slightly bowed legs. 'Come with me,' he commanded, taking me by the back of my neck.

He took me, on that day and others, to the broad expanse of lawn outside. I would stand, trembling with a fear that I could smell in my nose, at the edge of the flowerbed. And wait. 'You must watch,' he told me. 'Watch it all the way into your hands. You got me? Don't blink.'

And then he would hurl the ball: oval, dark, a dangerous shape of leather. It hissed toward me through the late afternoon, an embodiment of all that was most frightening to me, and all I could never do: I dropped the ball. I turned my head in fright and it would glance off my blunt hands, spinning away into the flowers. 'Sorry,' I cried. 'Sorry, sorry... '

I ran to fetch it.

'Give it up, Dad. Don't even bother.'

This from Malcolm, who would sit on the lowest step of the veranda. And laugh.

'Leave me alone,' I said, as much to my father as to him.

'That's enough, Malcolm,' Dad said.

And kicked the ball at me. This time I caught it: by some chance it found its way into my hands. I tossed it carelessly back again.

'Well done,' Dad said encouragingly.

'That was lucky,' Malcolm whispered.

'Leave him, Mal.'

I can still see my brother as he was on the step that day: sunburnt, sulky, his hair too long. He could catch any ball that was thrown at him. He was captain of his rugby team at school. He couldn't spell or do sums, but he had a rebellious spirit that couldn't be quashed. He kicked stones, with his tie pulled down and the top button on his school shirt undone. He carved his name into the wooden desk-tops in the classrooms and swore savagely and spat expertly sideways. He had a yellow mark on his first finger and thumb from smoking. He was my father's son. I was the impostor, with my mother's dark eyes; while Malcolm had Dad's icy stare.

The two of them played ball together on the lawn outside. It wasn't an awkward exercise with them; it was truly a game. They practised passes and tackles, stitching lines of movement that tied them invisibly together. Malcolm could kick and catch the ball on the run. Sweating, grimacing with pleasure, they would come back indoors together afterwards, arms around each other, luminous with pride and effort.

'Your heart,' my mother warned, from above her sewing.

'I know,' my father gasped, one hand on his chest. 'Where are my pills?'

For myself, I don't believe he had a heart at all, this swollen, implacable man with his shirts open to the belly, showing his gold chains and bracelets. Everything about him, even the most casual details, was expensive but somehow cheap. I don't know what smallness he was trying to compensate for, but he gave off an endless energy and size: he was loudly generous and bullying and expansive. His voice seemed to come from some deep recess in him, always on the verge of insincere laughter, wreathed in the blue smoke of his Cuban cigars. He was full of tricks and trinkets and finery. I had never seen him naked. His hands gestured hugely on the air. He was, by nature more than by vocation, a millionaire.

I have never understood exactly what my father's business was. But it had something to do with the stock market and, more recently, with pieces of property all over the country. He owned plots of land here and there along the coast; he had entire blocks of flats in his name in Cape Town and Johannesburg. On the walls of his study, between the disembodied heads of animals that he had deprived of life, were cryptic certificates framed in gold. One of these – a big, ordinary looking bit of paper – was the deal that had started his career. 'The one that made the difference,' he told us, beaming. I knew I was supposed to be impressed, but it was just a boring sheet of jargon to me.

Since that first big deal, my father had made a lot of money. As he never tired of explaining, he 'worked to stop working'– by which he meant he was rich enough to retire. Not entirely: but aside from the few hours each day that he spent on the telephone or at his unseen office in town, he was usually somewhere around the house, cleaning his guns, or wallowing in the pool, pulling himself with huffing strokes through the water. But he didn't look at ease in these long, idle hours. No, what he wanted more than anything was to be away, out of town, in the bush somewhere, and it was often that I came home from school to find the house all empty of his presence, streaming with light. On such occasions my mother would be happier than usual. 'Your father is away in the swamps again,' she would say, a small subversive smile flickering on her mouth.

Or: 'He's gone to the Eastern Transvaal for some shooting.'

Or fishing in the Transkei.

She had long ago decided that these outdoor trips were too rough for her and opted to stay at home, with me and a squadron of servants. So he went off with a bunch of men for company, loud and hairy and intense, like him. Most of them were people he did business with, for whom the savagery of nature was a metaphorical substitute for the world of money. They congregated at our home sometimes, before or after these trips, wearing designer outdoor gear, drinking beer and *braaing* steaks on the lawn. They were, and behaved like, people in no doubt of themselves, laughing unrestrainedly and slapping each other violently on the back. They had names that underlined their natures: they were Harry or Bruce or Ivan or Mike. There was Fanus, whom I had caught pissing in the roses once. I was afraid of them and went out the back door to avoid them.

When he turned fifteen, Malcolm would go with my father on some of these trips: from time to time there was a double absence when I returned from school. And though I was deeply relieved that I had never been called on to go too, I was jealous of my brother. He would return from these odysseys flushed and voluble, so eager to boast that he would even lower himself to talk to me. He would come to my room sometimes, late at night when the light was off, and tell me stories about things that I could only imagine. 'I drank red wine,' he said once, 'till I vomited out the window of the Land Rover. Dad wouldn't stop, he just laughed at me.'

And somewhere deep down in myself I longed to vomit out of windows too, to earn the laughter of my father.

Or the time he shot his first impala. 'It wasn't dead, it was lying on the ground, kicking. Dad killed it with a knife.'

I nodded solemnly, entranced and appalled. The knife was at my throat.

In the end I asked my father if I could go too. It was a

rash, impulsive request, and after he agreed happily, swelling with pleasure, I was filled with bitter regret. But somehow the next occasion came and went, and I stayed behind at home. I was learning the taste of relief and jealousy mixed together, a taste like ash. It was a taste that sprang quickly to my tongue whenever my brother was around.

Malcolm was strong and splendid and mean. He behaved as though he was immortal. So his sudden death wasn't just painful and tragic, but somehow against the natural order of things. He died in 1986, when I was seventeen years old, in my second to last year at school. Malcolm had failed matric and gone straight into the army.

He was made for that uniform. He looked casually handsome, capable of heroism and brutality. And if he had died a soldier's death, in a hail of bullets, or a purifying baptism of fire, it might have been less terrible and terminal. But he died in an ordinary traffic accident, in an army jeep somewhere on a nameless stretch of road. A burst tyre, a skid, a ditch at the edge of the tar.

He was given a military funeral. I stood between my parents – my father rigid with grief, my mother sedated – as the coffin, vividly draped with the South African flag, was lowered into the ground. I jumped when the rifles fired. And the next week at school there was a special assembly in honour of my brother, after which the other boys came to shake my hand in grim commiseration.

What I myself was feeling at that time I have no idea. I see events, and myself in them, from a distance. It is a story told by dolls or puppets, on a strange, unreal set. I do remember seeing my father cry for the first time in my life – shaking, soundless sobs unleashed into his hands as he sat drinking whisky at his desk – and the feeling, though perhaps that came at a different moment, that it would have been better if it had been me that died. There was the knowledge, too, that I was carrying a heavier cargo now, of guilt or transplanted hopes. And the dread of failure.

I thought that the heaviness was mine alone, but none of us was the same. Malcolm's absence left a larger void behind, which drew us ineluctably into its dark. In whatever secret place it is that human lives are welded together, joints and seams had been pulled out of place. All the unhappiness that had been squashed down under a lid suddenly boiled over into open view.

Within four months my parents were divorced. My father kept his house and I moved out with my mother. I visited my father over weekends sometimes. Almost immediately he started to shack up with a series of girlfriends, the first one being his secretary. It had never occurred to me that he might have lovers, not even on those long trips out of town, and I was shocked. But none of them ever stayed long; some of them were replaced between one of my visits and the next. I don't think he was especially attached to any of them and it took me a while to work out that it was a form of mourning for my mother. They were all substitutes, each temporarily, glossily, inhabiting her space. At the same time he became over-solicitous and concerned about me – another kind of substitution.

My mother also changed, radically and suddenly, but in the opposite direction to my father. She, who had been so devoted and submissive, threw off the role of wife as if it had been weighing her down. 'I feel like myself for the first time, Patrick,' she confided in me a few days after we had moved out from my father. 'It's all been an act till now.' And I saw that she had undergone three very different incarnations in her life. The first was that of the photo on the wall at *Ouma*'s place: a little Afrikaans girl on the farm, with pigtails and a missing tooth. Then came the young, pale wife, shorn of her past, eddying in a beautiful vacuum. The third, which started when my brother died, was the one that possessed her now.

She said that she had finally become a real person, but who she really was remained a mystery out of reach, even to herself. As if through the years of her marriage she had been holding herself painfully static, my mother gave in to motion. This was obvious on a physical level: she was constantly restless, looking around her, moving about. But her condition ran deeper than this. She threw herself with wild abandon into different fads and movements, and then discarded them for others. She took up diets, she played with different styles of clothing, she joined clubs and societies for two weeks at a time. She ate only red meat for a while, then became vegetarian. She joined Greenpeace. She campaigned for animal rights, standing in the rain on street corners with placards and grisly photographs. And from animals she moved on to human beings: for the first time in her life she became passionate about politics. One of the things she held against my father was his patriarchal brand of capitalism. She joined the Black Sash, the End Conscription Campaign, the Detainees' Parents' Support Committee. She became rabid and incoherent on the subject of the Crossroads carnage. I listened – at first with amazement, later with resignation – to the rhetoric of liberation.

I realised quite soon who the real victim was. Taking on the cause of this group or that, being vocal at meetings at rallies, she was actually making a plea for herself. *Look at me*, she was saying, *I'm here, notice me*. And as time went by she began to look like one of the dispossessed and vanquished on whose behalf she was supposed to be fighting. Gone were the dresses and makeup of her wifely years. In their place came jeans and *takkies* and T-shirts emblazoned with slogans and patches and dirt. I had never seen the skin of her face before, with its subtle blotches and mottlings. She didn't shave her legs and armpits anymore. She put on weight, then lost it again. In the end she came to resemble, uncannily, the staring, maimed dog in the anti-vivisection poster above her bed.

Along with these changes, of course, there were lovers. A lot of them, not all of them male. She changed partners almost as often as my father did, but her motivation was entirely different: while he was genuinely in mourning for her, my mother never looked back. There were hippies and solemn accountants, radicals and students. The only type that never passed through her bed again was the slick businessman that might have reminded her of her ex-husband. No, that was the past; and the future was defined purely by how enthusiastically she could give herself to everything she had never done before.

It wasn't long before drugs entered the picture too. I was too alarmed by now to follow the development of this scenario. It started with marijuana, the smell of which filtered out of her room from first thing in the morning, but rapidly progressed to all sorts of other, more dangerous chemicals. Usually these were taken in the company of her friends, the odd, transient characters that were always drifting in and out of the house in those days, like a kind of vapour. But on one occasion I came home to find her alone, lying naked in a comatose trance on the floor. I shook her and shook her, but it was a long time before her bony face stirred and lifted, whorls of shadow clinging around her eyes. In that moment our roles reversed: she became the lost child, holding on to me, desperate for consolation and meaning. I could only cradle her in revulsion and pity.

In the morning she was better. She squeezed my wrist at the table and said, 'Hello.'

'Hello.'

'What we both went through last night. Thank you, Patrick.'

'That's all right,' I said, though it wasn't.

'I'm glad, actually. It's brought us together. Pulled the walls down a little. We need to get all the inhibitions and bullshit out the way. We don't need secrets from each other.'

'Yes,' I said, but I wondered then whether people don't need their secrets. Lives are meant to be separate and apart; when the borders break and we overflow into one another, it only leads to trouble and sadness.

My father, who had never been so separate and apart from her before, was watching all this from a distance. He questioned me about her whenever I saw him. He did this in a cautious, roundabout way, not wanting to seem too interested. 'And your mother,' he would say, after he'd asked me at laborious length about myself. 'How's she doing?'

'She's all right, I suppose.'

'She doesn't look all right to me. She looks unhealthy.'

'Really,' I said. 'I hadn't noticed.'

He stared at me for a moment, then down into his whisky. He poked reflectively at his ice with one finger. 'That guy she was with when I dropped you,' he said. 'Is she seeing him?'

'I don't think so,' I answered, and probably it was true: by then she would have chucked him for somebody else.

Once he had an idea. Laying a comradely hand on my shoulder, he said: 'I'm going hunting in Zambia next week. You want to come along?'

I mused on this for a while, then said: 'No, I don't think so, thanks.'

'What do you mean? You'd enjoy it, Patrick. You should give it a try.'

I paused to savour my cruelty. 'Killing things isn't my idea of fun.'

He blanched with suppressed anger. 'That's not the point, and you know it. It's about being outdoors, under the sky... ' He shrugged. 'Why am I explaining? Malcolm didn't need it explained.'

'I'm not Malcolm,' I said.

We changed the subject then and talked about inconsequential things. But both of us knew that we'd skirted close to the edge of a very deep abyss. I didn't visit as often after that and he stopped asking me about my mother for a while.

He'd kept Malcolm's room preserved almost exactly as it was when he'd died. The bed was always made up, the curtains opened in the morning and closed at night, as though my brother was away on a short trip and might return at any moment. On the walls and table were perhaps twenty or thirty pictures of Malcolm, a whole chronology of his life, from being a fat scowling baby to the sulky young man in uniform.

Then I went to the army myself. I went reluctantly, too young and unsure to face the alternatives. I had no real idea of what lay ahead; just a sense that it was utterly at odds with my nature. But I thought that the sooner I went into it, the sooner it would be behind me. I didn't know at that time how certain experiences are never past, even when they are behind.

My mother wrote to me, long self-obsessed letters in which she only sometimes remembered to ask me about myself. She talked about the journey she was on, the journey to discover herself. I was losing all sense of who I was by then, but I didn't know how to give voice to the gathering absence. Instead I wrote short notes in reply, terse accounts of military life, and then stopped writing altogether. But she didn't seem to notice. She went on with her monologue. She was trying her hand at acting again, 'the creative life that marriage killed in me.' But she wasn't confident enough, or there wasn't enough work, and she only ever landed a few little parts here and there. She was battling for money. So when an old friend, installed in a lecturing post up north in Namibia, invited her to come up to the academy to fill in for somebody else for one term, she accepted immediately. It was a change from the usual, she said, and she was a junkie for change. She went to Windhoek to teach drama, and that was how she met Godfrey. And that was why we were making this particular trip now, into the past – hers and mine.

# CHAPTER THREE

I woke to the sound of a pig being killed. I sat up rigidly in bed, not moving till the noise suddenly stopped. Then I got up and dressed and went outside.

I had forgotten this about the farm. Its calendar runs on slaughter: Tuesday morning, the pig; on Wednesday, a sheep; on Friday, a goat. In between all these, at arbitrary times, any number of chickens meet their fate. All of this death to support human life: the flesh goes into our bodies, to keep us alive, to keep us going.

Animals are killed in different ways. There are specialized methods according to which each one meets its end. When I was younger, my mother had brought me up here for weekends and holidays, and I had watched many of these executions with appalled fascination. Chickens had their heads chopped clean off with an axe. Goats and sheep had their throats cut. They were led out to a patch of bare ground below the stable, where they were pinned down to the ground, their heads were pulled back and their arteries opened. What horrified me most was the mechanical indifference of the killing, the impassive face of the man who held the knife, which contrasted obscenely with the panic of the dying animal. Chickens were the most frenzied: they ran around insanely, spouting blood. The sheep were the most docile. They stood almost stupidly as they bled, watching the world fade away.

Pigs were a different matter. The pigs had their legs trussed up and were rolled onto their backs. Then a thin filament of iron was pushed into them, into the heart. It was, it is, a highly skilled task. In all the years of my childhood I had only ever seen one man doing the pig-sticking: Jonas, old even then, his face all shattered with lines, who would come out of his room, bent forwards as if with the inordinate weight of his duty. He prodded a little with the tip of the metal rod, divining the exact spot, the heart. Then, like a picador, he would throw his frail weight behind it as he drove it in.

There is no sound on earth like the sound of a pig dying. It is a shriek that tears at the primal, unconscious mind. It is the noise of babies being abandoned, of women being taken by force, of the hinges of the world tearing loose. The screaming starts from the moment the pig is seized, as if it knows what is about to happen. The pig squeals and cries, it defecates in terror, but nothing will stop its life converging to a zero on the point of that thin metal stick.

I had always, as a child, been deeply disturbed by the sound, but I could never keep away. Whenever a pig was killed I was there, among the watching black children, in the first rays of sun, with my hands over my ears. And afterwards I followed the trail of the carcass as it was dragged bloodily to the barn, to be butchered.

It was a sign of my state of mind or soul that on this particular morning the screaming of the pig sounded almost beautiful to me. It didn't evoke violence or fear, but a train of gentle childhood memories. Soft-focus memories, moments on the farm.

But when I came down to the barn, the noise was over and the cold dawn air was crystalline with stillness. And some of those childhood memories carried over to the present: the sun was coming up and over the trees in the orchard, just as when I was young; the mist was dissolving. Near the labourers' houses there was the same mob of black children scampering in the dusty arena; as though they were the same and I – I alone – had grown older, they went completely still and waved at me. I waved back.

There was a man standing nearby, very black, his teeth vividly white in his face. When he saw me he whipped his cap off his head and said, '*Môre, Baas.*'

I gestured abruptly, dashing away his servility, but he misunderstood and looked cowed.

'The pig,' I said. 'Where is the pig?'

He pointed to the barn. Framed by the door like a painting, the glowing carcass hung upside down, suspended from hooks in its legs, dangling in a way no pig was meant to do. Strangely colossal, amplified in death. And next to it was the figure of a young black man, maybe the same age as me. He was wearing dirty overalls, blotched with maps of dried blood. On his feet, also stained, were galoshes. In his hand, a long silver knife.

I came closer. He raised his head, watching me with sullen eyes.

'*Waar is Jonas?*'

He didn't speak. He raised a long arm and pointed over my shoulder, into the charred brown veld. When I turned back in confusion he said:

'*Dood.*'

The single syllable dripped from his mouth. Then he turned his back on me, and went to work on the pig. The blade punched down with delicate violence and in a moment I was watching as complicated guts, parcels of organs, came tumbling to the ground.

The stench of it – deep, bilious, foul – hit me. I took a step back and found myself in motion, stumbling away through the killing ground, where the marks of the dragged carcass showed like cryptic signs in the dirt. Down the hill, past the cramped laager of workers' huts, to a dry field where little cartridges of earth marked the sites of numerous graves. There were no headstones, no plaques. On some of them a little cross of wood had been planted and on some of the crosses a name had been burned out in black. Here and there were wilting bunches of flowers.

It was to this dusty plot that the young man had pointed; and I found Jonas's grave at the western edge of the area, in an exposed patch of ground. It was one of the newest. Stuck into the earth next to his tiny wooden cross, the iron pig-sticker was planted: rusting quietly, trembling gently in the breeze, an aerial sending signals from the grave.

I stood there for a while, but there was no emotion, for me, in being here. I walked on, to the far side, where a wrought-iron fence marked off another cemetery – the real cemetery, the white one. It was a neat, delineated garden, screened off discreetly with trees. I opened the gate and went in, to my grandfather's grave.

He had died a year before, while I was still in the army. I was up on the border. I received the news from my commanding officer, who told me with sibilant sympathy that my *Oupa* had 'gone to the sky'. This officer had also told me, in almost the same breath, that the funeral had already taken place the day before. 'So there's no point in you going down.'

'But why wasn't I told?'

'I only heard this morning.'

'But why, Commandant?'

'I don't know, Rifleman. Messages take long in the bush.'

I reeled out in a daze from his office. I hadn't been close to my grandfather, but I was shaken by this news – maybe because it brought back to me the memory of a world beyond this mad, hermetic one in which I was trapped. Later, on sentry duty at the gate to the camp, I suddenly started to cry. Astounding my fellow guard, who knew nothing about what had happened, I found myself saying, over and over, 'everything goes, everything goes.' It was this sudden insight into the transitory nature of things that unmanned me, rather than any personal affection for *Oupa*.

He was a white-haired, fierce old man who made everybody around him afraid. He had been a farmer his whole life, with something of the reddish colour of his fields in his skin. He had never made a tender gesture towards me or my mother. I had seen his teeth in a glass next to his bed at night; this confirmed him as immeasurably old, an impression that was only deepened by his old-fashioned style of dressing, in khaki clothes with a waist-coat and boots, a leather whip under his arm. On Sundays he dressed up in a worn brown suit and drove into town to go to church. We were forced, when I was small, to go too. I can still smell the damp, stony fragrance of the pews, from which prayers lifted up like heat.

Now he was dead. I stood at the foot of his grave. There were thirteen or fourteen of these mounds inside the enclosure – unlike the tired hillocks on the other side of the fence, all carefully trimmed and tended. Granite headstones, gravel paths. Each grave was topped with a slab. I read the inscription on his headstone: PETRUS JOHANNES DE BRUIN 1921 – 1988. Fresh flowers leaned in a vase.

This was the family cemetery; cousins, aunts, brothers, lay nearby. Next to my grandfather, his parents were buried; on the nearer side was an open place; in time, I knew, my grandmother would lie there. It was continuity, succession, links in an ongoing chain leading out of the unknown past, all the way down to me. The thought coupled somehow with the image of the pig hanging in the barn and, feeling suddenly queasy, I went back out through the gate and carried on walking away from the house.

Through the orchard, down to the well. This was about half a kilometre from the house. It was getting on for breakfast and I could see a line of smoke rising from the chimney. By now my mother would probably have come to my room to wake me. But I didn't want to go back. Not yet.

The well wasn't in use anymore. But there was still a circle of dark water below, which I could see when I leaned forward over the edge. With the sun at the right angle, not reflecting off the surface, you could sometimes see frogs in the water, drifting greenly in space. And now a memory came to me, of hunting those frogs, with a little coloured girl, my playmate from my early years. Her father was one of the workers on the farm. But to me Margaret was an equal, a companion provided by the strange spaces of the farm. She wore soiled cotton dresses and men's broken shoes. She picked her nose and the scabs on her legs. We wandered around the countryside together, finding things to amuse us, only parting at the end of the day when it was time for me to go inside the big house again. I loved her as much as my age would allow. Looking down now over the edge of the well, I saw a picture of Margaret and me, tense and trembling with excitement, eyes shining, as we lowered bread-covered hooks on lines of thread. A twitch, a pull, and in a moment we had the frog: a struggling fistful of slime.

There was a flat rock nearby – our operating table. We would lay out the frogs on their backs and cut open their bellies with a sharp piece of glass. Unzipped, exposed, their tiny hearts beat for our gaze. This innocent cruelty spun my mind around, half in shame, half in joy. Where was Margaret now? What had happened to her?

Other memories tumbled into my mind, also let loose somehow by the sight of the dead pig that morning. Nearby was a windmill, broken, lopsided, disused. And I remembered a day when a cormorant – exhausted and lost, far from the sea – had landed on one of the sails to rest. Cormorants struggle to fly, they need space in which to take off, and on this particular day a wind came up and set the windmill suddenly moving. Margaret and I, at work on our frogs, had turned to the sight of a bird dropping cleanly out of the sky. We ran to it, frightened, with our frog-bloodied hands. It died on the ground as we watched.

Another memory: this one nearer the house, on the old see-saw. Margaret and I were playing, going up and down in a regular, gentle rhythm. Near us, on the grass, two dogs were mating. They were mongrels that belonged to the workers; bony, sick-looking creatures. As they staggered around in their weird dance we paid them no attention; we had seen it before. All around on the farm, in between the death that we casually inflicted, life was making more life: cattle and chickens and pigs were all at it, a rampant, blind, voracious rutting.

All at once, from the back of the house, my grandfather came running. It must have been Sunday, because he was dressed up in that brown suit. He had his whip in his hand and for a terrified instant I thought that we were the object of his fury. But it was the dogs that he fell upon, spastic with rage, lunging and swearing in a hot vortex of dust. The dogs ran for cover while the old man still lashed about at his own shadow. Then, muttering softly, he stalked back inside, trailing the leather behind him, not looking at us.

Margaret and I stared at each other as our movement – up, down, up, down – went mindlessly on, getting slower and slower. We didn't speak a word. But later that same day, as dark was coming down, we found ourselves at the river. There was an overhang in the bank and we squeezed in underneath it. Without consultation, as though it was planned – and I saw now that it followed on from the dogs that morning – we started to touch each other. We put our hands under clothes and explored.

It didn't last long. On some signal again, we each retreated, pulling our hands down to our sides and sitting staring at the water sliding past. But then shame rose in me and I said to her:

'You don't tell. Do you hear?'

'I won't.'

'Because I'll get you into trouble. You hear me? I'll get you into big trouble.'

She was crying now. 'I won't tell anybody.'

Inspiration came to me, a first intimation of power: 'My *Oupa* will fire your father. I'll tell him to throw him out.'

'No,' she said. '*Asseblief.*'

'*Moenie sê nie. Moenie sê nie.*'

'*Ek sal nie.*'

'You and your father will have to go away.'

We walked home separately then. I was ten years old. Though I came back often to the farm after that, I never played with her again.

The shame of that day, which I hadn't felt at the time, only touched me now. The memories, that had been flowing and falling with such ease into the present, suddenly stopped. I was not a boy anymore; I was a man on a different mission. And I was late for breakfast.

They were still at the table. 'Where have you *been*?' my mother said.

'I went for a walk.'

'Do you want to eat?'

Without waiting for an answer, my grandmother rang her little bell. Anna came in, still without shoes, carrying a tray. I sat down to a plate of bacon and scrambled egg and toast.

'Everything you're eating,' *Ouma* said, 'comes from the farm. Even the bread. I baked it myself this morning. Do you want some coffee?'

'Does that come from the farm too?' my mother said.

I poured coffee for myself.

'You must eat, Patrick,' *Ouma* said. 'You must put on some weight. Look at him, Elsa, how thin he is.'

'You sound like Howard when you say that.'

'Look at him.'

'He's always been like that. You just don't remember. It's been a long time since you saw him.'

'Of course I remember how he looked. He's lost weight, can't you see that?'

It was uncomfortable for me, sitting there like a skinny object in the middle of their discussion. There was some kind of tension between them that had nothing to do with me. I said, 'I'm eating, look at me, I'm eating,' and they both went quiet for a while. Then my grandmother said:

'Where did you say you're going to in South West?'

'Namibia, please.'

'South West,' *Ouma* repeated doggedly. 'It's always been South West Africa.'

My mother sighed. I wondered whether *Ouma* had caught wind of our real reason for going, but she would never have let an issue like Godfrey pass. There would have been a colossal drama, followed maybe by eternal silence, not just this unspoken prickliness at the breakfast table.

'Windhoek,' my mother said. 'Just for a few days.'

'I don't know why you want to go there now. They're having that trouble up there.'

'Trouble? What trouble? They're having elections now, that's what they're having. Democratic elections, the first. That's not trouble.'

'It could be dangerous, Elsa. What do you want up there?'

'I want to see the elections. It's a rehearsal for ours down here in a few years.'

*Ouma* made a clucking noise of contempt and took out her pipe. As she filled it and tamped down the tobacco, I relaxed a little. If there was going to be an explosion, the cue had just passed. My mother was always baiting *Ouma* with these little political hooks, and there had been some ugly scenes in the past. It didn't get us anywhere, this vicious friction around the table; it was like a personal revenge for my mother, for the way she'd been brought up, the values that had been taught to her as normal. But she would never change my grandmother; it was too late for that, and maybe it had always been too late. *Ouma* was made of a different material than us city people. I looked at her now: a small, dried-up old woman, with a heart like a dark clod of earth. Since her husband had died, she had taken over the running of the farm. All the lines of power radiated outwards from her. The servants were afraid of her. The neighbours respected her. She couldn't be separated from the land that she lived on.

She puffed on her pipe. A peaceful mood overtook her and she became lost in thought. 'I went up there once.'

'To Namibia?' I said.

'South West.'

'When was that?'

'Long ago. *Ek kan die jaar nie onthou nie*. I went with Petrus. I remember the sand,' she said dreamily, 'there was a lot of sand...'

In the silence that followed, we were all of us lost in the sand.

Abruptly, the question rising from nowhere, I asked her: 'What happened to Margaret?'

*Ouma* was startled out of her reverie. 'Who?' she said. 'I don't know a Margaret.'

'She was a friend of mine,' I said. 'When I was a boy and I came here for holidays – '

'Come on, Patrick,' my mother said, suddenly impatient to get going. 'It's late already, we have to make a move.'

I went upstairs to get packed. In half an hour we were playing out last night's scene of arrival in reverse: my grandmother took me by the shoulders to say goodbye, while my mother closed the boot on our suitcases. 'Come again soon,' *Ouma* said. 'Remember to eat, Patrick.'

My mother kissed her quickly on the cheek. Then she got into the driver's seat and started up the engine.

'Have a nice time in South West.'

'Namibia,' my mother said. 'Namibia.' She let out the clutch too fast and we sprayed a wide circle of gravel as we wheeled around and started up the drive. I looked back, waving, but the solitary homestead, with the old peasant woman in front of it, had vanished already into the wilderness.

# CHAPTER FOUR

It was with a sense of definite unease that I crossed over the frontier. After six hours of driving, by which time we were drugged with the heat, we came to the border post. Two sluggish fat guards came to meet us. One, tugging an Alsatian on a short length of chain, circled the car like a planet. The other, bored, gave us some forms to fill out. He examined our passports and stamped them, then he lifted up the boom and waved us indolently through.

Under the bridge the green of the river was startlingly vivid in contrast with the colourless land all around. On the far side we came to another border post. Again the two guards, overflowing with ennui, almost like brothers of their fellows over the river. Again the forms, the questions; then the white boom lifting and the same-looking countryside opening out before us.

It was both strange and utterly normal to be back. I had been in this country – South West Africa, Namibia – ten months ago. I had been posted here for almost a year; it would probably have been two if what happened to me hadn't happened. But I'd never been here, so far south before: I was familiar with the north, which was a different landscape to this. The north was grassy and full of trees, almost lush in places, while this was a dry, bare, stark terrain, close to desert, which gave way in an hour or so to dry bush, studded with outcrops of stone, ridges of rock.

My mother was tired; I drove, while she lay and dozed in the back. It was very hot by then. A white fist of sun clenched the car and wouldn't let go. My hands were slippery on the steering wheel. I turned the radio off and a silence came down, inseparable from the numb, yellow, empty land outside. There were no people. We passed an occasional railway-line, or shack, or car, which burst like noise out of the violent, dead silence and then passed away again.

As we went further, there were small signs of human life. These are poised, in my memory, in sharp relief against the hazy ribbons of heat: a youth slouched under an umbrella, with his hat pulled down over his face. A pair of donkeys, coshed by the sun, standing pointlessly harnessed to a cart. Performing in miniature the more historic trek of colonial pioneers, we came to Windhoek in the evening. Under a cooling sky we descended into a basin among the hills, and the buildings, the streets – after all the emptiness – were like a kind of explosion. Steam rose from the pavements, among the jacaranda trees, and I drifted for a while among the visions of houses, each one set in its little rectangle of sand. I stopped eventually next to a wall, on which somebody had splashed words in red paint: *SWA IS 'N VRYSTAAT!*

'Mom,' I said. 'Hey, Mom.'

She woke, dazed, wiping streaks of hair from her face. 'What? What's the matter?'

'We've arrived,' I said.

# CHAPTER FIVE

My mother had booked us into a hostel on the edge of town. It was a new, ugly building, in a garden with trees carrying white blossoms that gave off a sweetish smell. The whole place was full of UNTAG officials, here to monitor the elections. We were given ID cards and keys and shown to our rooms by a balding white man in shorts, who kept apologising in a whiney, nasal voice; he was sorry about everything, from the overcrowded lounge to the colour of the carpets.

'Sorry about the view,' he said, as he unlocked my room.

'The view' was of a township across a big open patch of veld, a vista of crowded tin shacks and fires burning in barrels. On the far side I could see empty grasslands stretching away.

'This is the smaller room,' he said. 'There's a bathroom through there. I'm afraid you'll have to pay in advance. Sixty rand a day.'

'You said fifty on the phone.'

'It's gone up – sorry about that. The whole city is full. You won't get cheaper anywhere.'

My mother opened her mouth to argue, then changed her mind. She paid tiredly, digging the cash out of her bag. As he went off, rolling the notes up like a cigarette, she called out to him: 'A telephone! Where's a telephone, please?'

'There's a payphone downstairs in the foyer.'

'I'm going to call Godfrey,' she said to me.

'We've only just got here.'

'I know, but I told him I'd call. I said we'd all have dinner tonight. There's a nice German restaurant near the academy.'

'Maybe I'll just stay here. I don't really feel like going out.'

'Don't be silly,' she said sternly. 'You can't leave me alone. I depend on you, Patrick.'

'You don't want to be *alone* with him? What are you talking about? He's your *boyfriend*.'

'You're coming for dinner,' she said. 'It's final. We won't be out late. Come on, you'll like him. We'll have fun.'

When she'd gone I started to run a bath. While the water gushed into the tub, sending up clouds of steam, I sat on the edge, feeling weary and worn out. Suddenly and without apparent reason, a familiar sensation started up at the base of my belly, spreading outwards to my arms and legs. It was a spasm, a shaking, a shadow passing over my soul. These little episodes had come to be referred to, in the language that had evolved between me and my doctors, as 'attacks'. My attacks were part biological, part psychological, and they tore me up like a thin piece of paper. My teeth chattered. My bones vibrated. I perched on the enamel rim, trying to assuage my grief. I was oppressed and horrified by things. The angularity of objects. The symmetry of tiles.

Then it was past. I turned off the taps, took a Valium and slipped into the bath. As the hot water and the drug took effect, I grew gradually calmer. I lay limply until my mother came in, smiling to herself.

She ran a hand through my hair. 'Dear Patrick,' she said. 'My baby.' But I could hear from her tone that she was thinking about him, not me.

'Was he home?'

'Yes. We're going over now. Don't go all lame on me, darling. I'm not taking no for an answer.'

I didn't want to meet Godfrey. In some way I was afraid of him. I had seen a lot of lovers pass through my mother's bedroom: young and old, men and women, the only thing they had in common was their transience. None of my mother's affairs lasted long. No doubt Godfrey would go the same way, but till now he had managed to achieve a certain mythic presence by virtue of distance. The fact that he lived here in Windhoek, so far from Cape Town and our normal lives, made him different and somehow powerful.

There was also the small matter of his colour. For all her experimenting and openness, my mother had never had a black lover before. I'm not sure why; she had broken a lot of laws already in her newfound political phase. But he was a first for her. And as with all her previous relationships, she was looking for something beyond Godfrey, some idea that he represented. She had been talking a lot lately about being African – about being connected to the continent somehow. But these declarations about how *rooted* she felt, about how much she *belonged*, sounded more plaintive than proud. I think there was a big psychological barrier that she had to overcome before she could get involved with him. On some deep level she was still a little Afrikaans girl on the farm, being watched and judged by her father and mother, maybe even by *my* father. And now she'd got past it; she'd freed herself.

My mother – since she'd got divorced – told me everything. I was her confidant and friend. We discussed topics from menstruation to masturbation, so the details of her romance with Godfrey were hardly taboo. I knew how they had gone to bed together for the first time after she'd been up in Windhoek for two months. He was in his final year, one of a five-strong class. From the very first, she said, she'd been aware of his presence, but not because she found him attractive. On the contrary, he had a rude and off-putting manner with her. He did his best to show how bored he was when she was teaching. He yawned and fidgeted and looked around while she was talking, which had the effect on my mother of drawing her attention entirely, exclusively to him. The game developed as the weeks went by. He came late for class, he stared out of the window, he treated her like dirt.

'And this excited you?' I asked.

'No, not at first. It infuriated me, it made me angry.'

'And so?'

'And so nothing. He kept on like that. The atmosphere was unbearable. Then one day I stopped talking and confronted him. He said he would speak to me after class. He waited when everybody had gone, and then his whole attitude changed. He was quite nice, actually. Sort of

44

sheepish and sweet. He said he was falling behind. I was going too fast for him. He said he needed some extra classes and could I help.'

'So you did.'

'Not immediately, no. I could see what he was after. I wasn't interested at first. He was... I don't know, too earnest. Intense.'

'So what made you change your mind?'

'Persistence, probably.' She thought about it and said, 'Yes, persistence.' Here she leaned forward and pressed a long-fingered hand to my arm, filled abruptly with earnestness of her own. 'Let me tell you something, Patrick. In this world you can have anybody you want, absolutely anybody, if you just focus exclusively on them and keep at it. Don't waver, don't let your attention slip. People will come round to any idea, even an idea they hate, if you persist. Persist. Don't ever give up.'

So Godfrey persisted. Everybody in the class knew; by then the tension was palpable. And when she eventually gave in and invited him to her room for an 'extra lesson', what followed on was inevitable. The sex that first time was stupendous, she said. 'Like an astral fuck, Patrick, if you know what that feels like. He banged my head against the wall at one point. I still have the bump – here, give me your hand.' And she made me feel the oval lump on the back of her skull, like a secret badge.

Things calmed down a little after that, but still their affair was intense. She was leaving soon, so time was limited. On top of that, liaisons between staff and students were illicit, so all their encounters were furtive and charged with danger. They coupled in cars or out in the open air

DAMON GALGUT

sometimes. There was always a rough edge to it, a touch of the violence of that first time.

'What do you mean, violence?' I said cautiously.

'Well, not *violence*, really. Not like you think. I just mean... he's not soft. He never kisses me, for example.'

'Never?'

'No. And he won't let me lie close to him afterwards. He's quite cold. It's hard to get any feelings out of him. But that's his background, you know. The kind of life he's led.'

When she got back from her time up north, she was full of new energy and enthusiasm. I could sense it from afar, in the letters she sent me up on the border. She didn't tell me about Godfrey – not till I returned home – but she was full of that new talk about being in harmony with the continent. And when she did eventually give me the full story, she wanted me to believe that sleeping with Godfrey 'was a political act'.

Despite all this nonsense, she did look very happy. There was a radiance in her face that I hadn't seen before. That she felt so good made me feel good in turn. I was partaking vicariously in this elemental connection; this contact she'd made with the earth. After the military twilight I'd recently been through, I also needed union with Africa. I didn't understand her esoteric jargon, her talk of belonging and peace, but I liked seeing my mother in this state, and I didn't question it too much.

I also didn't believe she would see him again. I knew her too well, and how her big passions faded quickly away. He was a radiant idea, but after he'd phoned for a few weeks she would get bored, meet someone else, and this particular phase would be past. So I happily joined in her plans to go back up to Windhoek to see him, never thinking for a moment that it might actually happen. It was just talk and fantasy, nothing real. But after a year, a year and a half, had gone by, the phone-calls were still coming, and the talk was still the same. And even so, when the first free elections were due, and my mother declared that there could be no more fitting time to go back up to Windhoek, I still didn't entirely believe her.

It was only now – now that we were actually here – that the idea had become fact. Maybe this was true for her as well as for me. Thousands of other people had come here for the elections, for the first true day of freedom, but we were here to see him.

While my mother was in the bath I sat on my bed, the light off, watching the under-lit spectacle of the township through the window. It was a scene you would never find in any upmarket white suburb: the dogs running around, the little groups of people in the street, the dirt and drunkenness – the raw vitality of it all.

My mother took a long time to get ready. When she eventually emerged she was wearing make-up and perfume, two things she had sworn on principle never to use again after she'd left my father. She simpered and twirled around for me to see. She had on a green skirt and sandals and a white blouse. Around her neck was a string of pearls that I dimly remembered my father giving her after he came back from an overseas trip somewhere. And it was only after we had crossed the yard to our car and were driving through the sultry streets again that I noticed she had shaved her legs – another broken covenant.

Though full night had fallen and there were clouds in the sky, the heat was unbroken. 'God, it's unbearable,' she said, dabbing at her neck with a hanky. The headlights in the car were erratic and at night she always crouched over the wheel alarmingly, as if in preparation for disaster. As we went she pointed out places of interest on either side: 'the administrator general's house,' she told me, 'the police station... that's the way to the airport... '

Godfrey wasn't a student anymore; he worked for SWAPO now. We were going to fetch him at his house, which was in the township. The view I could see from my hostel room window included the road we were on now. There was a clear dividing line where Windhoek came to an end and Katatura began; as we crossed over this line I said to her, 'Are you sure you know where we're going?'

'Of course I'm sure. I've been here hundreds of times. You don't have to worry, Patrick. It's perfectly safe, I promise you.'

I'd visited perhaps three or four townships in my life. A few times, when I was small, I'd been with my father when he drove one of his workers home. But those trips were distant memories and belonged anyway to another point in history: before 1976, before Soweto happened. In recent years, of course, the townships had become war zones. These days the soldiers that weren't sent up to the border were sent to the townships instead – a different sort of border. Somebody from my matric class at school, a boy I hadn't known very well, had been killed in one of these township battles.

Although they were usually invisible, the townships

were always close by. They encircled our cities like besieging battalions. They were always just out of sight, over a rise, behind a hill, discharging smoke and noise and a daily cargo of flesh. Buses and taxis came in and out, trains rattled in their guts. The newspapers at night carried stories of the terrible things that happened in them. We'd made them what they were, then despised them for what they weren't. They were a negative print of our lives.

Godfrey lived in an untarred little street, with tiny houses clustered close together like clams. There were no pavements, no lights. We swerved around a group of boys playing soccer in the gloom, who seemed utterly uninterested in us, then passed a horse that was ambling aimlessly, and pulled up at a house like any of the others. There was a warm breeze stirring as we got out. Perspiration pricked out the line of my spine. I followed my mother through a lopsided gate, across a dusty yard, to a tin door. As we were about to knock a skeletal dog came running at us, but it was tied to a chain and couldn't come close. Only after it jerked up short did it start to bark – furiously, manically, but somehow without passion.

The door opened suddenly. Godfrey was a short, squat figure in a red T-shirt emblazoned with a SWAPO slogan. He looked completely impassive, but then suddenly smiled at my mother and put out a hand to squeeze her arm. Just that: the small gesture of greeting; and I remembered what she had said about how cold he was. But the effect was tender, and when he shook my hand I could feel how much soft warmth came through his big fingers.

'Come in,' he said.

I followed my mother, who followed him, into a small

kitchen. The walls and floor were bare concrete. There was a table with a plastic cloth on it and an old woman sitting on the other side. She had a cataract in one eye, and a blue cloth tied around her head, and her expression didn't visibly alter when my mother went to embrace her effusively. 'This is Elizabeth, Godfrey's mother,' she said. 'My son, Patrick.' The old lady sat stiffly, her arid hands on the table playing with a small, orange pen. The colour of this object, its anomalous presence, drew my eyes down to it, but she just kept turning it in her stiff hands.

We sat, while Godfrey brewed a pot of tea on an electric plate. He performed his alchemy in silence, while my mother chattered anxiously about the long drive up here, the heat, the excitement in the air. Then, as he thumped two smoking mugs down on the table, he said abruptly, 'Andrew Lovell's been killed.'

'Who? Oh, him, God. What happened?'

'He was shot. I heard just now. Somebody in a car, they have no clues.'

'That's terrible. I can't believe it.'

'Biscuit?' Godfrey said, holding out a tin.

'I've lost my appetite. Have a biscuit, Patrick.'

'Who's Andrew Lovell?' I said.

Godfrey's eyes settled appraisingly on me. My mother said:

'He was an activist, darling. He worked for SWAPO.'

'Who shot him?'

'Don't be so ignorant, Patrick. South Africa did it, obviously. Some undercover agent, one of their hitmen.'

'But why?'

'How can you be so naïve?' But she didn't explain. She

sipped her tea and looked at Godfrey, her gaze softening sentimentally. 'Are you hungry yet?'

'I have to go to Swakopmund,' he said.

'What? When? Not *now*... ?'

'Not now. In the morning. Andrew was organising a rally there, I have to take over from him. And there is going to be a memorial service.'

'God. Swakopmund. This is very sudden.'

'Is your car okay for the trip?'

'My car... ? We're going in my car... ? Yes, it'll be okay.' She became peevish as the inconvenience of it hit her. 'I thought we were going to stay in Windhoek. I don't want another long drive.'

'I'm sorry about that. But this is what's happened. We'll be back in time for the elections.' He was looking at me again. 'Maybe Patrick would like to stay here.'

'No,' my mother said, 'he can't stay on his own. He'll come along. You'll like Swakop, darling,' she assured me, 'it's very pretty. On the coast, north of Walvis Bay.'

'I know where it is,' I said. 'I was in this country before, remember?'

I'd spoken sharply, but the silence that followed was more watchful than angry. Godfrey shook the biscuit tin and said, answering her earlier question, 'Yes, I'm hungry. Let's go.'

On the way out the dog came running out of the darkness again. But this time its rush was friendly; Godfrey went down on one knee to pet it. And as he looked up at me, grinning, I saw that he was just a young man, not much older than me, who also, perhaps, felt a little shy and awkward in my company.

\*

The restaurant was up a winding staircase, on a sweltering balcony, jammed with umbrellas and people. My mother had told me that it was a site famous for local revelry, that had only recently opened its doors to all races. The manager, an anaemic German with a lick of blond hair, fussed us to a table at the far edge, overlooking the street.

'You would like wine?' Our Aryan host smiled tightly.

'Beer,' Godfrey said.

My mother ordered a bottle of wine for me and her. She had recently become vegetarian again and she wanted only a salad to eat. Godfrey ordered a steak, and – after a hesitation – I followed him. Then she and Godfrey slipped into a closed conversation, whispering to each other and giggling, while I leaned on the railing and watched small events in the street. The wine went straight to my head and turned my tiredness into lightness: it felt pleasant to be here.

They were busy re-connecting after their long break, smiling coyly at each other and rubbing hands. There was a lot of sexual energy in the air. He didn't seem cold to me – there was no reserve in the way he touched the back of her neck, or draped his arm possessively over her shoulders. Their mutual absorption allowed me to study him properly for the first time. His skin was deeply and strikingly black, making his big teeth seem vividly white. His hair came down into a sharp widow's peak in the middle of his forehead.

When the food came he transferred his attention from my mother to his plate. He ate voraciously, with single-minded attention. She was just getting warmed up to the game and was a little put out at being neglected in favour of a steak. So she turned serious:

'What's the mood in the country?'

'The mood? Can't you see?'

'Well, we only arrived today. It's hard to draw conclusions.'

'People are happy,' he said shortly, and went on chewing.

'It's a big moment,' she said.

'Sure. For us, it's a big moment.'

'Not just for you, Godfrey. For the whole continent. It's the beginning of the end, we all know that. South Africa's going to follow soon.'

He made a snorting noise that could have been agreement or dismissal, and ordered another beer. My mother was miffed and soon after went lurching off to the toilet. Godfrey and I were left alone together for the first time. We tried not to look at each other.

He gave a soft belch. 'So,' he said.

'So.' I smiled. 'I know your voice from the telephone.'

He smiled too, but he wasn't going to follow this line of conversation. 'You said you'd been here before.'

'Not to Windhoek. I was up on the border.'

'Yes. Fighting.'

'I wasn't much of a fighter,' I said.

He adjusted his T-shirt, so that I could see more clearly the image of the clenched fist, the slogan. I wasn't sure whether I was being baited, or whether the talk was innocent. I had no desire to talk politics, much less the politics of the South African war on the border. I said:

'I had a little crack-up there. I don't know whether my

mother told you about that.'

He was watching me, and I noticed he had a fleck of blood in the corner of one eye, such as one finds in a fertilized egg. He seemed about to answer, but then my mother came back and the conversation veered off in a safer direction.

There was a heavy storm brewing as we drove back to the hostel. Lightning fizzed high overhead, throwing the streets into sharp relief – streets usually struck into torpor by flies and dust, now full of frenzied activity. Even late at night, cars and people were moving everywhere. From remote and forgotten corners of the country, from points on the globe I could hardly pronounce, soldiers, officials, observers and voters converged in gathering droves. Bunting lined the streets. Election posters crammed onto poles and trees. YOUR VOTE IS YOUR SECRET. VOTE FOR TRUE PEACE. I THINK THEREFORE I VOTE. SWAPO flags and DTA banners, bits of graffiti, discarded leaflets. The feeling was poised somewhere between a party and a riot.

At the hostel the night guard gave us a cursory glance and let us through. But as we walked over the grass I saw somebody watching from behind a curtain. My mother was quite drunk and making a lot of noise, screaming with laughter and hanging onto Godfrey's arm. She kept telling us to keep quiet, though we weren't making a noise, and then going off into fits again.

We hadn't even got to our rooms before the bald man, the manager, was there. 'I'm afraid we don't allow visitors after eleven,' he said. 'It's a rule, I'm sorry.'

My mother was suddenly sober. 'He's not a visitor,' she said. 'He's staying the night.'

'You didn't make a booking for him.'

'It's my room. I made a booking for my room.'

'I'm sorry. It's not allowed. This is a same-sex hostel.'

'A same-sex hostel,' she said, 'or a one-race hostel?' She was icily furious and I could see there was a scene coming.

'Mom,' I said. 'Just leave it. Why don't you go and stay at Godfrey's place tonight?'

'This kind of thinking,' she said, 'will be history soon.'

The bald man was going red, but the moment – and the scene – thankfully passed. 'All right,' she said. 'I'll go and stay somewhere else with my *boyfriend*.'

It took her a while to pack her overnight bag. Then she came and touched my cheek and said, very seriously, 'Patrick. You don't mind, do you?'

'Mind what?'

'Me going. You'll be all right on your own.'

'Perfectly fine,' I said, but I wasn't sure whether this was what she'd really wanted to ask. There was a weight to the little question that made us both feel uncomfortable.

'We'll come and get you in the morning,' Godfrey said. 'Sometime after breakfast.'

She started to say something else, but by then Godfrey was manhandling her, all angles and skin, through the door. She waved once, weakly, then I heard her renewed giggling floating up the stairs.

Abandoned in the passage, I felt suddenly desolate. That innocuous fluorescent light, those slippery tiles, were the shore of a strange foreign land. I heard the car start up below, drive off.

I went to my room and sat there for a while. I knew that I couldn't sleep, despite my tiredness. On the floor below, some UNTAG officials were having a party; I heard music blaring. Outside, the lightning sizzled.

Then – though I hadn't planned it – I went to phone my father. It was after midnight and I woke him up, but I could hear he was pleased that I'd called.

'How you doing, Patrick?'

'Fine.'

'The drive okay?'

'Yup.'

Then, because there was too much to say, we didn't speak at all. In the pause, lightning flickered again; I could hear its burr on the line. I found myself saying:

'Dad, she's... '

'Is she with him?'

'Yes,' I said. 'They've gone now.'

My father made a noise: maybe just a swallow, but it sounded like a tiny glottal cry. For an instant, joined by a thousand kilometres of umbilical line, the telephone united us both. I opened my mouth to speak, but at that moment the storm broke outside. The phone went dead in my ear.

# CHAPTER SIX

I'd been posted to the border in April the previous year, along with thousands of others: a rankless, nameless number. After basic training I was flown in a Dakota to the far north of South West Africa – now Namibia – and deposited at the side of an airstrip in the bush.

Our camp was miles from any recognizable settlement. We lived out our lives between shades of brown: our uniforms and tents, and the colour of the landscape in every direction. For most of the time that I spent in this camp we didn't do very much except keep ourselves going. Most of us weren't patriotic, but we were obedient. We were like a nomadic, inbred community, obsessed with ourselves. Our tribe was the army, our secret rites and rituals were tribal: we made our beds, we stood inspection, occasionally we did PT under the eye of a bored corporal. For the rest we lay around in the tents, playing cards, writing letters, telling jokes. An old scene, as old as the first village.

We thought for a while that we would never see war. But there is a certain terror in waiting. Perhaps only I felt it so acutely: the ennui and aimlessness, in which the overpowering *maleness* of the place started to suffocate me. It was the first occasion in my life that I had been in a group of men, with not a single female face. More to the point, it was the first occasion I'd been away from my mother for any length of time. It was like being with my father and his friends in an isolated hunting lodge, deep in the swamps somewhere, for months and months and months. Except that it was only the officers and permanent force members who were older; most of these men were my own age, just out of school. But even they – or especially they – were inscrutable and strange to me: laughing, jostling, testosterone-swollen animals with whom, it often felt, I had nothing in common.

And I didn't know why we were there. Some of the others were true believers, but even the rest seemed to have some clear notion of what our function was. To me the camp, and the hard, harsh land that surrounded it, were inexplicable torments, designed exclusively for me. I don't mean I didn't know about the politics. I had been hearing about the border for years already; so much so that it had become a mythical site in my head. It was like the edge of the world. Beyond it, as in ancient maps, was where monstrous and unknown things dwelled: Communists. Terrorists. Other Ideas.

I knew all that; I mean something different. On some other level, now that I was actually *there*, my presence ceased to be a political act and turned into something else. It turned into an existential test, a contest of endurance between my soul and the material world around me. None of it was real; the thorn trees and grass and termite hills and jackals and barbed wire and boredom and huge, vacant sky were just a set, loaded with dangerous props and hostile extras. All of it to stage my downfall.

*

Four months after I arrived, there were two new arrivals in the camp. The first was a thin young man called Lappies. He was a rifleman, like me. Lappies – we knew him by no other name – was tall with white hair. His one eye was grey, the other one blue; they made his face seem out of balance.

He was posted into our tent. He slept diagonally opposite me on the other side. We couldn't help but see each other when we woke up in the morning or went to sleep at night, or lay on the bed, composing letters home. I noticed him in a way I hadn't noticed the others. I noticed the shape of his shoulders, the thin covering of almost invisible hair on his chest.

We became friends. I'm not sure how this happened: there was no particular event, no significant occurrence to connect us together. We weren't even especially similar: he was Afrikaans, from a farm near Potchefstroom. But somehow we sensed a certain common ground between us, though neither of us would have given it a name. It was a feeling more than anything – a feeling of being at odds with the world we found ourselves in. Then the feeling led to small incidents of exchange or chat; I borrowed his iron from him one night; he borrowed a shoe-brush from me. We landed up in the bathroom together one night, sharing a mirror as we shaved. It was the first normal, easy conversation I'd had since I arrived. I remember he actually made me laugh.

The companionship deepened, went further. There were no big confidences traded, no pledges made, but something had started. We took walks around the perimeter of the camp and talked about our families, our school years. Lappies had a girlfriend back in Potch. He showed me photographs of a bland girl in plaits who worked, he told me, in some government office. As time went by he told me other things too, stories about his family, his life before the army. We got on well.

The other arrival was more frightening. His name was Commandant Schutte. Like Lappies, he had white hair; this feature aside, he resembled, disturbingly, my brother. He had a big moustache and a confident swagger and a scornful laugh. At certain angles, in certain lights, his resemblance to Malcolm was startling. It made a crack in my heart.

Commandant Schutte was in charge of the camp. His predecessor, a pimply captain who'd been too soft for the job, flew out the day after the commandant arrived. From that moment on nothing was quite the same again. The lazy air of aimlessness was wiped away at one stroke. Schutte was a soldier to the core – a mean, hard, meticulous, obsessive man. For the last few months it had been possible to forget that we were in the army at all. That illusion was now dispelled: PT became a daily occurrence again. Inspections, which had been lackadaisical and perfunctory, took on the mad, merciless quality they'd had in basic training. Idlers and slackers were punished with detention or courts martial. An atmosphere of purpose and fear descended onto the camp.

In the mornings now, we had to assemble and stand at attention while the South African flag was raised. Then we sang the national anthem, staring rigidly in front of us. Afterwards we were put at ease and Commandant Schutte talked to us. These daily addresses took the form of lessons. Sometimes they were religious in nature, for the commandant was a re-born, unwavering Christian. More often, though, they were fierce homilies on the nature of the enemy 'out there'. Because he wanted us to know, without any doubt, that the enemy was real, that he was watching us, that he would never rest till he defeated us or was killed. That was the choice: him or us. And the idea of the enemy being victorious was unthinkable. The enemy was everything that the commandant – and by extension, we – were not: he was communist, atheist, black. If the enemy won, our country was finished.

I did not care about the commandant or his invisible, insidious enemy; but it was hard not to be part of the new energy that took over the camp – and harder still not to feel afraid. All the other men seemed to have been infected by it. The bush wasn't an existential backdrop anymore; it was the cover and camouflage for forces bent on our destruction. Closer to home, though, it was the commandant I was really afraid of. He was a far more palpable enemy than the black soldiers hiding in the grass, and far more dangerous to me personally. It became my neurotic terror that he would find me out – find the secret weakness in me. Because my weakness was the flaw in the dam wall that held the enemy at bay; I was the tiny chink in the armour through which defeat would come flooding in.

I had no doubt that if the commandant could see me, see me for who and what I really was, that his revenge would be swift and terrible. So I hid. I tried to blend into the ranks, do everything that I was told, so as not to be obvious or conspicuous. I didn't want him to notice me, not even for a moment. I kept my head down. I didn't foresee the spotlight searching for me in the particular way that it did, picking me out in the middle of an ordinary, arbitrary afternoon.

Commandant Schutte believed in sport as a way of keeping fit and building a team spirit among the men. He told us so in one or two of the morning lessons, but the idea remained abstract. Until one day when we were told to fall in, divided into groups of fifteen, and set to playing rugby on the parade ground.

It was terrible. It was like being a boy again, hopelessly overcome by the world. And at the same time there was nothing boyish about it: the contest of knees and fists and will on the baked, cracking earth was elemental, old. I couldn't catch the ball. As on those long-ago days on our green urban lawn, I fumbled, I dropped it, I blushed. Now, however, I couldn't cry; grinning bravely, I endured their scorn:

'Winter, for fuck's sake!'

'Winter, you *doos*!'

Commandant Schutte stood at the side, observing from above his white teeth.

I discovered I had a friend. Lappies, in a pale froth of sweat, dropped the ball as often as I did. As though it was a fruit, newly skinned and slippery, it burst out of his hands. His lantern face trembling, twitching with terror, Lappies danced around.

'Lappies, go back to the farm!'

'Lappies, *jou moer*!'

The Commandant smiled.

After the game, silver with sweat, Lappies and I stood apart. We slapped each other on the back, pretending a heartiness neither could feel.

The next time a rugby game was announced, nobody wanted to play with us. The teams formed up quickly, and we were left alone. It was a bewildering moment, but it didn't last long: the Commandant came quietly up to us. 'You two,' he whispered, smiling tightly, 'are on guard duty.'

So on that day, and on all the other rugby days that followed, we walked around the edge of the camp. It was a small camp, and from almost no point along the perimeter of the fence could we not see the game in progress.

Our segregation confirmed what had always been sensed. The others kept their distance from us now. They treated us kindly, but also remotely; we weren't part of the team. We were apart. And there was a certain relief in having been discovered. The pretence wasn't necessary anymore, with all the toil and angst it entailed: the mask had dropped. There was a brotherhood of men, I now clearly saw, to which I would never belong. My father, my brother, the boys at school – they knew things I didn't know. There was something in their hands that helped them to catch balls in flight. More than that: it was beyond me to participate in their rituals of kinship. I would never hunt animals in the bush, or stand around a fire with them, beer in hand, tugging at my moustache. I was pale, I was weak, my jokes made them blanch. I would never be part of their club.

I remembered my brother, sitting on the step:

'*Give it up, Dad. Don't even bother.*'
'*Leave me,*' I whispered. '*Leave me.*'

Soon after Commandant Schutte's arrival, bloodshed came to the border. As though the war was somehow intimately connected to him, the violence suddenly blew up in his wake. For the first time there were SWAPO incursions into our area; for the first time there was talk of walking patrol.

Then one night, without warning, there was a mortar attack on the camp. The conical shells hissed in out of the dark and ripped craters out of the ground. The first one landed close to our tent. I didn't know what was happening at first; there was the rush, the sound, a rain of dirt coming down on the canvas. I found myself under the bed, pressing my face into the ground, wondering if I was already dead.

Another explosion. Another. Then silence returned, rolling in from the bush like a different kind of concussion. Not even the insects were singing. Then the human hubbub started – voices, feet running, engines starting up. Someone – a soldier like us – had been killed by that third shell.

So the fighting started. Our lonely camp, which had been, till then, the site of rugby and boredom, was suddenly on the front line. All the talk of patrols finally turned into action. We were formed into squads and sent out into the bush for six days at a time. Sometimes we set out from the front gate, sometimes we were taken out in a helicopter and dropped. The aim was simple and terrifying: walk as quietly as we could, looking for the enemy, and kill him. The enemy was also walking, like us, or sometimes he was hiding in the local villages. He had to be burned out, exposed, executed. He had to be cleaned out like a cancer.

We saw this enemy soon. Some patrols brought prisoners in, their hands held over their heads. So the enemy had a face now. It was human, this face, with a black skin, and an air of fear or dejection not very different to ours. But if I felt sorry for the enemy, my compassion was quickly washed away in the flood of activity and stories that rushed over us suddenly. There was a lot of talk, now, about fights in the dark, about bullets and battles. Sometimes whole patrols didn't come back, or came back in the form of one or two babbling, shattered survivors.

Body bags were on perpetual order now. They were used mainly for our men, who were zipped up and flown home, to their wives or families. The enemy was usually just left in the bush, or piled up in holes and covered unceremoniously in a thin layer of soil.

I was very afraid. I didn't want to leave here in a black plastic sack. I didn't want a military funeral like my brother, or a special assembly in my honour at my old school. One night, outside the tent, listlessly tossing stones, I said to Lappies:

'What are we doing here?'

He frowned and shook his head.

'I don't know anything about SWAPO,' I said. 'I don't hate these people. I'm just here for two years because I have to be. It's a law. I might have to shoot them – that's a law too. They might shoot me, but at least that's because they want to. But I don't know why I'm doing this. It's got nothing to do with my life.'

Lappies looked around furtively. 'Shhh,' he said, 'don't talk like this.' And it was true: this talk was seditious. I could be punished for this talk.

'I want to go home,' I said.

'Don't think about it. Don't think so much.'

'How can you stop yourself from thinking?'

He shook his head again, threw a pebble and got up. I had gone too far, I had driven him away; but after he'd started walking he came back and sat again. 'I hope I don't have to kill somebody,' he said morosely.

I walked a lot of patrols, but by luck I had only one contact with the enemy. We were going in a line through the veld, following the corporal in charge of our mission, heading back to camp. It was close to the end of the day and somehow the fading light, the proximity to safety, made it seem improbable that anything could happen. So it was a deep shock when we came around a low hill and walked into them, a group of five.

For a moment we stared at each other – just two little bands of men who'd bumped into each other in the wilderness. They seemed as startled and astonished as us. Maybe somewhere in space light has preserved the image of that moment, suspended and infinite. But on earth the moment passed. We were suddenly fumbling with rifles, cursing and running.

I have tried, in letters that were censored down to gibberish, to explain this encounter to my mother: how it felt to be shooting at other people, trying to kill them before they killed us. But words don't do the job, really.

Language falls short of the reality; it only gives you the surface. How I threw myself down in the grass and aimed and shot. I saw – from where did it rise up, that image? – a leopard on an island of wood. It went on for ever, or five minutes, full of smoke and noise and, from somewhere, the distinct smell of shit. Then it was over and those of us who were left got up to our feet and walked on weak, shaking legs.

We killed four of them, and the others ran away. They killed one of ours. The bodies lay on the ground, as if they were just resting, as if they would get up in a minute and walk away. I have no idea, and I don't want to know, whether I was responsible for any of those deaths. I was shooting into a blue void, into a screen on which action was being projected. None of it had anything to do with me.

But I stood over one of the bodies, the one closest to me, and stared at him with mesmerised horror. Maybe I had done this, it was possible. The face was already stiffening. He was young, younger than me. Just a boy, really. His eyes were open, but furred over with sand, which gave his stare a soft, unfocused quality. He wore his death with a kind of indifference, as though it didn't affect him.

'Well done,' Lappies said, coming up from behind and putting his hand on my shoulder. 'Did you get him?'

I nodded, and then shook my head, but he didn't say anything else. We just stood there, looking down. I could feel his hand trembling.

The corporal cut off all the SWAPO ears and put them into a bag.

On the next night, back at base, Lappies and I were on guard. A cuticle of moon hung over the trees. As we trudged round and round on our lonely, circular vigil, we didn't talk. We were both heavy with what had happened to us the day before. I don't know how it happened, how we stopped, who touched whom first – but at the darkest corner of the camp, we drew together. We were suddenly fumbling with buttons, slinging down our rifles. I remember his breath on my neck. Standing pressed together, the immensity of the continent spreading outwards as though we were at the very centre of it, we took each other in hand. A few seconds of gasping and tugging and pulling, like a subtle wrestling match, and it was done. We left silver tracks on the ground. Then we buttoned ourselves and went on our way, not able to look at each other.

That was one year ago. Now I had returned to Namibia – to the country that I had lost myself in defending, which was being given away in a week. It would go, almost certainly, to SWAPO, the terrible communist enemy who could never be allowed to win. But they *had* won, and the world was still on its axis.

With my mother and her lover – who had been, for five years now, one of those enemies – I carried my bag out to the car. My mother travelled with a heap of suitcases and Godfrey had to make two or three trips; meanwhile I leaned against a wall in the sun and she came to lean next to me.

'What are you thinking?' she said.

'Nothing. I was just remembering somebody.'

'Remembering who?'

'Just somebody. Nobody you know.'

It was another blazing hot day. As promised, my mother and Godfrey had come to get me after breakfast. They didn't look as if they'd slept too much last night. I said to her now:

'How was the historic reunion?'

'Historic,' she said with a wicked laugh. 'Worth the drive up by itself. How was your night?'

'Quiet,' I said. 'I slept.' I didn't mention the short talk with my father.

Godfrey came out with the last luggage and loaded it up. He was wearing the same angry T-shirt from last night, as well as a pair of black shorts and slip-slops. He said to my mother, 'Is he coming to the SWAPO offices?'

'Why shouldn't he?'

'I don't know. I thought he might prefer to wait.'

It took me a moment to realise that this abstract third person they were referring to was me. 'He'll come along wherever you're going,' I said. 'He doesn't like being left behind.'

'I have to get some posters and things. For the rally.'

'Okay.'

We drove slowly through the hot streets. There were fewer people out, and they kept to the shade. Some of them made signs as we passed: clenched fist for SWAPO, forked fingers for the DTA. We went into town and parked in a side street not far from where we'd eaten last night. The SWAPO offices were on the second floor of a bland, brick-faced building. A security grille covered the entrance. Godfrey spoke into an intercom and we were let through, into a foyer with a lot of aimless people waiting around. There was a SWAPO flag on the wall, with a photograph of the SWAPO president, bearded and beaming, next to it, hung slightly askew. All this bureaucracy, with its ordinary, dusty tedium – it seemed so very at odds with the black men out in the bush who'd wanted to kill us. This was like any government office back in Cape Town, like civil service officialdom anywhere in the world. We passed down a long passage, to a room whirring with the commotion of printing presses and piled up with stacks of posters and leaflets. A tiny black man in a white coat was in charge. He called Godfrey comrade and looked very formal and serious for a moment; but then he broke out in a friendly grin and the two of them had a private conversation, full of nodding and jokes.

The posters we'd come to collect were waiting on the counter nearby. I studied them while we waited. Looking out at me, sketched in grainy black ink, was the face of Andrew Lovell. The photograph looked like an old one, taken years ago. He was thin, with dark hair brushed forward over a high forehead. Narrow cheeks, with a big smile, an intelligent glow in the eyes. Not a special, extraordinary face. A face not entirely unlike mine. Underneath it said, 'Comrade Andrew Lovell, 1960 – 1989'.

There were also piles of smaller hand-bills, printed on pinkish paper, giving a history of Andrew Lovell's life, under the heading 'Freedom Fighter'. The jargon was repellent and intriguing to me at the same time; I glanced through it and learned about Andrew Lovell – that he'd been born in Johannesburg and had lived there till going down to Cape Town to study law in 1979. He'd served on various councils and committees, most of them banned by now. Under the state of emergency he'd been detained and had spent several months in prison. On being released he'd gone to Namibia, where he worked underground for SWAPO. At the time of his death he was facing charges for refusing to serve in the army. His life, the pamphlet said, had been one of selfless commitment to the struggle.

Andrew Lovell had been murdered the previous morning in Swakopmund, at about the time we'd left my grandmother's house. He didn't live in that town – he had been based in Windhoek – but had been visiting temporarily while he organized an election rally. As he came out of the local SWAPO offices, he'd been shot by unknown attackers in a passing car. He'd been hit by a shotgun blast in the chest and had died on the pavement before any medical help arrived.

I didn't learn all of this from the pamphlet; some bits and pieces came to me later, from my mother, from the newspaper, from listening and looking around. But already that morning I had a clear sense of who Andrew Lovell was, of how very different his life had been to mine. And I had a feeling, somewhere in myself, of something approaching – though I couldn't say what.

When Godfrey had finished with his conversation we loaded ourselves up with the posters and pamphlets and carried them down to the car. The smell of fresh ink followed us all the way.

My mother and Godfrey were too tired to drive, so I was behind the wheel. 'I'll show you a different route,' Godfrey said. 'Let's avoid the main road.' Windhoek, in striations of colourless houses, fell gradually away from the car. We crossed over a highway that was still under construction – teams of black men labouring in overalls – onto a gravel road. Parched yellow grasslands opened around us, dotted with misshapen trees. The road passed through farms; we kept going over cattle grids, through big fields mapped out in wire.

Nobody spoke. In the rear-view mirror, her image broken by a fine crack in the glass, I watched my mother doze off. Lulled by the rhythm of the car, her eyelids slipped down, her face flattened out. In a while she had slumped against the door, mouth open, a vein pulsing in her neck.

Godfrey noticed her. He was sitting in the front seat next to me and a glance passed between us, followed by a smile of complicity. But after this little moment there didn't seem to be anything else to say. The silence went on. The heat and the dust were oppressive. The windows were closed, but a thin grit got into the car. It furred up my teeth, blocked my pores, invaded the joints of my bones. Outside the bush had given way to mountains of silica: folded, hollowed and haunted. The land was stripped down to its bones. The road wasn't level any more.

'Is this the desert?' I asked.

Godfrey shook his head. 'The real desert is still coming.' He looked at me for a long moment. 'You have never been here?'

'Not this part of the country. Only up north.'

'You didn't want to see this? The country you were fighting for?'

'I did want to see it. I wasn't fighting for anything. I was just... ' It seemed pointless to go on. Instead I said, 'Did you know him? Andrew Lovell?'

'Sure. He was a friend of mine.'

'What was he like?'

He thought about this for a while, so long that I thought he wasn't going to answer. Then he said, 'He was quiet.'

'Quiet?'

'Not shy, but quiet. Very intelligent. Good with words – a legal man. Not many jokes. A legal man,' he repeated. 'Do you want a cold-drink?'

Solemnly we peeled the tabs off our tins and sipped. What I wanted to say, but didn't, was that Godfrey seemed unaffected by the death of his friend. Perhaps, after all, they had never been close friends. Or perhaps this was the way of things when you were involved in a political struggle – people were killed, or people disappeared, and you had to go on. You kept your eye on the cause you were fighting for, but you didn't get too involved in the tragedy of the other soldiers fighting with you. Not a normal war; not a war like the one I'd been caught up in.

When we passed out of the hills, the land levelled into a flat plain, extending into a haze of heat in the distance. It was almost shocking – the vastness and emptiness of it. 'There,' Godfrey said, 'that's the desert.' There really was nothing growing. The sand looked like cinders.

'I want to stop the car,' I said.

'So stop.'

I pulled over. When the engine stopped the silence was immense and suffocating. We opened our doors and stepped out into the sand. Heat, light, dust: I leaned against the car. There was nothing to see, nothing to fix your eye on, unless it was the curve of the earth. Godfrey squatted down. He put one hand between his spread knees and pressed his palm flat into the ground. Just before he got up again, wiping his hand on his leg, I thought I saw his shoulders trembling gently, as though a voltage had passed up his arm. It was a curious gesture, and somehow sad.

When we got back into the car my mother was waking up. Wiping strands of hair from her face, she yawned pinkly, like a cat. 'Ooh,' she said, 'that was a nice sleep. Have you boys been taking a pee? Oh, look. We're in the desert. Isn't it something else, Patrick? A real trip.'

Several hours down the road, the desert changed again. From stone it became sand, soft dunes undulating on either side, creeping into the road. There was a curiously liquid quality to it, sliding and drifting and blurring. It was moving around in the wind, rearranging itself all the time, grain by grain. If you lay still it would form itself around you, take you into itself.

Just outside Walvis Bay we came to another border post. My mother sighed. 'It's South African territory,' she said. 'Show them the passports, be a sweet.' But the soldiers here weren't very interested; they glanced at our passports, peered at Godfrey and waved us through. I had the same unsettling feeling I'd had at the border down south: that the landscape itself continued without regard for the artificial lines marked out on maps. People died fervently, passionately, for their particular patch of territory, but the earth – in a certain sense – was somewhere else.

We skirted around the edge of Walvis Bay and followed a road up the coast. We were in a flat belt between the sea on the left and the weird dunes rising on the right. Pelicans stood like crowds of concerned citizens on the beach, staring gravely out across the water. We came to another border post - with again that same unreal quality, as though the boom, the booth, the soldiers and us were all floating a few inches above the surface of the earth – and then we arrived in Swakopmund. The sun was going down, and in the last reddish glow the big old houses, the spare Germanic architecture, were both elaborate and flimsy, like delicate but detailed screens that had been put up as a backdrop for some event which never quite took place. We were very tired. We drove around aimlessly for a while, then went to a hotel near the sea and booked ourselves into two rooms.

# CHAPTER SEVEN

Swakopmund was a town built on sand. It sprouted almost absurdly out of nothing, like a mirage on pale foundations. The edge of town was a disquieting sight, where the houses ended and the desert began. The transition was sudden and curiously violent, containing some kind of force. Humanity and dust, the old opposition, locked into temporary stasis.

A word here about the desert. One's brain will not see what is there. My eye kept registering a long ploughed field, in which rocks became houses or telephone poles. Some treacherous pocket of the inner sight tried to fill up the void with recognisable debris. It was almost painful to see – to really see – the vast, softly hissing nullity of it. The lines of houses were like a pathetic imposition of order on something beyond rules or chaos.

If you moved inwards, away from the edge of town, the illusion of permanence was greater. Some of the buildings were beautiful, made out of wood. The streets were empty and broad, lined with palm trees like tall, tropical sentinels.

The hotel – because no other would have taken Godfrey in – was a dirty little dwelling, mottled with damp. The rooms, though, were spacious and tidy. A television was blaring downstairs in the foyer, being watched at all times of the day or night by an assortment of tired-looking people, haunted eyes focused on the screen, drooping around dimly lit tables with checkered plastic covers. I have no idea who they were or where they came from; they were like part of the hotel. None of them talked, except for the manageress, an obese woman in a tent of a dress, who commented with her smoke-roughened voice on the action, while the rest of the audience emitted a murmurous wordless chortling in response.

Behind this room was the bar. This, with synthetic wood on the walls and threadbare mauve carpets underfoot, was lit in an aqueous green. Congregations of young people hung about the snooker table in the corner, cigarettes pasted to the corners of their mouths, hair greased wetly down. One of them, an elderly teenager, wobbled around on a wooden leg.

The woman behind the bar was hard-looking and bitter, her hair dyed blonde-white, her nipples permanently erect under her skimpy T-shirt. While she poured out drinks with no visible change of expression in her face, she told me in her metallic voice about how she'd been married in Johannesburg, but had headed out here two years before, to escape.

Many of these people had fled here from elsewhere. It was that sort of place. The wooden-legged man – not a teenager after all – was also a divorced South African, who'd come here to start a new life. The sprightly black man who helped at the bar had used to fight for SWAPO in Angola. He beamed when I tipped him, and the odd possibility crossed my mind that perhaps the two of us had shot at each other.

The new life that all these people had come here for wasn't much in evidence. It looked like a shadowy sort of half-life to me, this twilight existence on the western edge of the continent. Perhaps because of this – because the eyes I saw around me were the eyes of refugees and orphans – I felt oddly at home here. It was Windhoek, by contrast, that had made me uneasy. But now, for the first time since arriving in the country, I felt bold enough to explore.

Leaving my mother and Godfrey alone upstairs, I went out of the hotel and into the street. The air was heavy with salt. I walked down the road in the unquiet dark, across a small stretch of lawn, to the sea. The water was jagged and black, and a long pier jutted out.

I set off along the road of slippery planks. It didn't feel secure under my feet; there was an uneasy creaking. The pier was old and barnacled, full of weeds. At the very end, a long way into the water, beyond the waves, a dim bulb threw out a circle of light.

And I wasn't alone here. An old man was leaning against the rail. He seemed almost to be part of the jetty, rusting and raw, so that it was a shock when he suddenly turned to look at me. But his teeth were newer than the rest of him; he smiled in welcome, his mouth glinting gold. '*Abend*,' he said with a cough.

'Evening.'

There was a pause.

'I can hear from your voice you are South African.'

'Yes, I've come up from Cape Town.'

'Myself, I am German.'

'I can hear that too.'

Beyond this strange, misshapen figure, far out at sea, a

single ship was passing. Its light moved slowly in a line, drawing my eye, until it disappeared behind him. I noticed that the old man had a cane, with a gold-encrusted head. He flashed those teeth again.

'I lived here long ago.'

'Yes ..? Where do you live now?'

'For thirty years now I have been in Germany. In Böckwitz. There is a cake shop there,' he added, for no apparent reason.

'You've been away a long time.'

'Yes. When I lived here I was very happy, but it was time to go. I thought, when I left, that I would never come back. There was no reason to return, not even when I was younger. Now I am old, and I am visiting one last time.'

'Why did you come?'

'I have come to vote. I couldn't let it pass.' He came close to me suddenly, moving surprisingly fast, and laid out one claw on my arm. 'This could have been a great country,' he said. 'There was hope here once. But now it's all going down the toilet.' I could smell his hot breath on my face, a deep foulness passing over the gold caps of his smile. 'It is hopeless, but I have come back to vote,' he hissed, 'for us. For *us*.'

For a moment I was paralysed, not understanding completely. Then I pulled away from his hand. 'Not us,' I said, 'not me.' I started to walk away and then broke, in three steps, into a run. The sound of my feet echoed on the planks, rebounding from the sea underneath. I didn't look back. I was running from him – that gnarled, gold-toothed man – but also from that terrible *us*. I wanted no part in what it presumed. I wanted to leave it behind.

*

Back at the hotel, as I was crossing the shadowy foyer, a voice spoke a name that I knew. I stopped and turned, mystified for a moment, until I saw the television set. Then I sat down among the rustling, peculiar figures at the tables. On the screen was an image of a pavement, on which an outline had been inscribed in chalk. The outline was of a body. Its arms were flung out at its sides. One knee was drawn up, close to the belly; the other was twisted away. Though the sketch had no substance, it managed to convey something of that terrible, final spasm. Andrew Lovell – the smiling, distracted face on the poster – was reduced to a chalk outline on grey cement.

The image passed to a porcine police official. His brown moustache waggled as he spoke, giving comic emphasis to his plosives. 'A team of investigators,' he was saying, 'has been full-time on the job. It's too early to say for sure, but we hope to be making an arrest soon.'

An interviewer with a microphone: 'Are the motives for the murder any clearer than before?'

'Well, you know. A person like Mr Lovell, with his history, he's got a lot of enemies. A lot of people don't want him around. I can't really say for sure.'

'Is it political, is that what you're saying?'

He shook his head. 'I have no comment on that.'

Further, retrospective pictures followed: the team of investigators he'd spoken about, at work on the job. What it amounted to was a bunch of bored-looking cops crawling around on the ground in a sealed-off area. There was a flash of the entrance to the office where the killing had happened. In the background, on a neighbouring shop window, I saw the name of the street; I repeated it softly to myself.

Then we were back with a suave sports announcer; a pin in his tie caught the studio lights, twinkling out a bright signal in morse code. The death of Andrew Lovell came late in the programme, far down the list of important events of the day. I got up and crossed to the fat manageress, who was holding court in her usual place in the corner. She looked up as I approached, her tiny eyes even tinier with suspicion.

'Do you have a map of Swakopmund?' I asked her.

She pointed with her chin at the wall behind me. The map was bright and colourful: SWAKOPMUND, JEWEL OF SOUTH-WEST. I didn't know why I hadn't seen it before. As I turned to go, the fat lady clapped a webbed hand down onto my wrist and leaned in close. She pointed again with her chin, but upwards this time, to our rooms.

'That lady,' she said, 'is she your mother?'

'Yes.'

'And the man? Who is he?'

I hesitated, but then anger, like a slow afterburn from my encounter on the jetty, flared up in me. I leaned back towards her and whispered in a voice even lower than hers: 'He is my *father*.' We stared at each other in silence for a second and then she withdrew her hand. I straightened up slowly and moved between the tables to the map on the wall, to see where Andrew Lovell had died.

# CHAPTER EIGHT

A tiny star of blood. That was the only evidence I could find. Anything else had been cleaned up. The pavement looked much as it had on the television last night: grey, cracked and bland: an ordinary pavement.

It was very early, the shop windows all shuttered and barred. I had woken up before dawn. The room, full of stale air, was warm, and I went to open the window. Then I'd stood, watching the thin light seeping into the sky, summoning up buildings, streets, doorways, out of the thick sea mist.

When I dressed and stepped out of the hotel, all the street lamps suddenly snapped off, as if extinguished by my arrival. The air was cold and blurry with vapour. I walked slowly through the town, knowing, but not quite knowing, where I was going. It was easy to find the place. I had kept an image of the streets and the way they fitted together from the fat lady's yellowing map.

The SWAPO offices, like those in Windhoek, were unmarked and undecorated, except for a small plaque. A few posters were stuck near the door, but otherwise the building was blank. The chalk outline, the whole business of investigation, had gone. But something in me, an intuition, was sure. I walked slowly up the pavement, scrutinizing the grey cement, until I found the one clue that had been ignored. On the very edge of the street, that delicate red droplet.

I stared at it for a long time. A rich little flower, springing from the stone. Disparate, unattached to its surroundings. It had a strange life of its own. I tried to imagine this liquid, bottled up inside the body of Andrew Lovell, coursing in his veins, keeping his heart ticking over. The image opened another in my mind. I could see the small, empty street, full of early morning light, not unlike the light that was falling now. I turned and looked at the doorway. Andrew Lovell and a friend came out of the entrance. They were tired after a whole night working. They stopped on the pavement, talking together, sharing a cigarette. Their mood was happy. In a few days all the struggling and fighting would be over. What they believed in, what they had worked for, would happen: the election, with everything it meant: freedom for Namibia, the beginning of the end for white South Africa. Maybe it was this very event they were talking about as the nondescript car, which had been parked further down the street, started up and came slowly nosing down towards them. They didn't look up, they didn't see the faces of the men inside – not even when the note of the engine changed and the car suddenly surged towards them, revving furiously, so loud that the blast of the shotgun was drowned. Andrew Lovell's friend said afterwards that he thought the car was out of control and that he was witnessing an accident, so that there were no words for his shock when the car suddenly took off, tyres smoking, and he turned back – in dreamy slow motion, it felt to him – to find his friend lying on his back, a pool of blood spreading under him. It didn't seem possible. Andrew Lovell had been annulled and in his place there was already an outline in white chalk, both arms flung out, one knee drawn up, the other twisted away.

But he wasn't quite dead. Not yet. He died quickly, lying there on the pavement, while his friend ran inside to phone for help. I have tried to imagine what thoughts might have passed through Andrew Lovell's darkening mind. With the pavement an inch from his eyes, what images lit up his sight? Did he know what had happened to him? Was it all unreal, or did he reflect in some unnaturally lucid way on the meaning of his tapering life – and did it seem worth it? If he could have known it would end like this, so messily, so painfully, on a patch of dirty cement stained with petrol and footmarks, would he still have done it? Or might he have wished to be me?

I sat on that kerb. I watched the town stir.

At first there was nothing. Then a few figures came into view. All of them, at this hour, were black workers getting the day cranked up into motion: in overalls or aprons, they went trudging slowly past, none of them especially interested in this lonely white boy sitting at the edge of the street. Then a few cars drifted past.

Things were gathering pace now. In a few windows blinds were raised, and one or two of the shops were opening. Opposite me the shutters went up on a butchery, and it was the sight of this particular window – red carcasses hung in a row – that got me moving again. There was a pig, dangling upside down, and I thought of my grandfather's farm. I saw the surly black man, the torrent of slimy guts. Offended by memory, by those nude, hanging bodies, I got up and walked away from the small flower of blood.

But I wasn't ready yet to go back to the hotel, where I knew my mother and Godfrey would still be in bed. I wandered around the streets for a while, looking at everything. There were posters everywhere. They were stuck up in windows, wrapped around poles, splattered on walls – all of them, in one way or another, begging for a vote. In between the posters were United Nations bills, explaining how to fill out a ballot. In the main street a DTA meeting was in progress. Half of the block had been roped off with bunting, inside which a bewildered crowd was corralled like cattle. A pair of hissing speakers discharged a happy tune, which was strangely depressing – all this enforced merriment, so early in the morning. I stood for a while, trying to work out what it was that seemed so odd about these people. Then I realised: they were drunk. The liquor was being poured out, a toxic breakfast, at a table at one end of the street: oblivion in exchange for a vote.

I wandered on, to an antique shop nearby. It was full of bizarre objects, a lot of them found after being dropped in the desert, rubbed smooth and warped by sand and wind. Then there was colonial debris: German beer mugs, old photographs, cameras and lighters and Victorian toys. Amongst all this refuse from ten decades of human existence were other, more sinister things. Embroidered swastikas. Pictures of Hitler. Dog-eared copies of *Mein Kampf*. Some SS dress swords, glinting wickedly. And one piece of recent memorabilia:

the 1989 Third Reich double-edged weapons calendar.

A bad-smelling German man behind the desk said angrily, 'Can I help you?'

I thought of the old man on the jetty. I thought of him slightly differently now.

'No,' I said. 'I don't think so.'

I went back to the hotel. My mother and Godfrey had just woken up. They sat up next to each other in bed, both naked. My mother didn't cover her breasts, which hung a little tiredly. I saw that Godfrey was in magnificent shape; his torso was sleek and toned, a piece of statuary propped against the wall. I had a mental image – disturbing, for obvious reasons – of the two of them making love.

'Patrick,' he said. 'You're up early.'

'I couldn't sleep. What are we doing today?'

'I have to put up posters for the memorial service.'

'I want to help you,' I said.

My mother stared at me. 'He's putting up *posters*, darling,' she said, as if I hadn't understood properly.

'I know that. I want to help.'

Godfrey was also looking at me, with a guarded, watchful quality. Then he smiled. 'Have you had breakfast already?'

'Not yet.'

'I'm hungry. Let's go and eat.'

Downstairs in the foyer, we ate a greasy breakfast at one of the tables in front of the television set. Godfrey had become businesslike and serious. 'We go to the township after this,' he said. 'We put up the posters, we hand out pamphlets. We tell people about the memorial service. Okay?'

He was looking only at me as he spoke, ignoring my mother at his elbow. I could see that she was feeling left out; her mouth tightened in a familiar way. 'I don't know about this,' she said.

'What do you mean?'

'This wasn't what I came up here for. I came to be in Windhoek, to see you. This stuff with posters, that wasn't part of the plan.'

'It's why we came here, Ellen. You knew what the plan was.'

'I didn't have much choice, did I?'

Now he was looking at her, but with a cold glitter in his eyes. 'You do have a choice,' he said. 'You don't have to help, if you don't want to.'

'That's not what I mean... '

'I know what you mean, Ellen. Don't worry about it. Just do whatever you want.'

He spoke casually, but his tone didn't fool me, or her. She looked sharply away from him, though he wasn't looking at her anymore either; he was putting his fork down carefully on his plate.

I record this moment, because something happened then that only became obvious later. This is how endings begin, with insignificant gestures: a fork in a hand put down on a plate. A mutual avoiding of eyes.

From her place in the corner, the fat lady was watching. She had a strange smirk on her face.

So for the second time in two days I found myself in a township. This one was smaller than Katatura in Windhoek. The dirt streets were wider, and the houses were poorer.

Faces watched us from doorways and windows, from behind walls and fences. I suppose we were a strange sight.

We drove from place to place, then parked and got out and stuck the posters up, then drove on again. It was a tedious business. As Godfrey had said, we handed out the pamphlets and spoke to passers-by about what it all meant. I had expected people to be antagonistic or disinterested, but that wasn't the feeling at all: the feeling was supportive, humorous. As the hours went by I found myself in a happy mood. It pleased me to be doing this job, and to see the face of Andrew Lovell spreading around. When the posters were all up and only a few pamphlets were left, my mother yawned and suggested we go back to the room. But Godfrey wasn't quite finished yet.

'We're going to hand out these pamphlets to whiteys in town.'

'What, now?'

'Why not now?'

'I don't know if this is such a good idea,' my mother said. 'They might not like it.'

'It doesn't matter if they don't like it.'

So we went back to the town centre and waited on a corner. The first person to come along was an elderly white woman. When I tried to give her a pamphlet she waved me away. 'No more politics,' she said.

The next one was more vitriolic. He looked at the pamphlet and became instantly enraged: he lunged at me, swearing and spitting. I wasn't hurt, but I was shaken by the violence erupting suddenly from what was ostensibly a mild, middle-aged man in innocuous spectacles.

'You see,' my mother said. 'What's the point?'

But Godfrey was determined. The point, whatever it was, seemed buried beneath his expressionless face, set woodenly on some interior resolve. 'Go back if you want to,' he said. 'I'm handing these out.' We stayed, though neither of us did very much. He handed out pamphlets over the next hour. I felt my happiness of that morning diminish. A few – a very few – people accepted the pamphlets, but most weren't interested, or reacted with rudeness and aggression. One man gave Godfrey a handbill in return, which said, 'Only terrorists call it Namibia.' About our feet, like a weird confetti, crushed pamphlets collected.

Suddenly my mother couldn't take it any more. She knocked the remaining pamphlets out of his hand, so that they fell in a serene blizzard around us. 'I can't stand this,' she said. 'No. I cannot stand this!'

He stared at her.

'Look, this is crazy,' she said. 'We get the point, all right? I'm hot, I'm tired, I'm going to rest. Are you coming or staying?'

'I told you,' he said stolidly. 'Go if you want to.'

'Fine. I'm going. Patrick, come on.'

'It's okay,' I said. 'I'll stay here.'

She looked at me. It was another moment.

'Right,' she said. 'See you later.'

She stalked away up the pavement. Her retreating back, stiff and furious, wasn't unlike some of the people we'd offended with the pamphlets. Godfrey snorted as she started the car and drove off but his heart wasn't in it any more: not long after that he dumped the rest of the pamphlets in a bin. 'That's it,' he said, 'let's go.'

We walked back to the hotel, not speaking to each other. It was the middle of the day and very hot by now. We retreated to our separate rooms, but not long afterward I heard them arguing. It was just a noise, two tones in conflict, till I got up and pressed my ear to the wall, and then their voices came through, dimmed slightly by brick:

'What do you expect?' she was saying. 'What do you expect me to do?'

'I don't expect a lot, Ellen. Just have some respect. The people in this country have suffered.'

'I know that. Do you think I don't know that? What can I do about it?'

'Don't turn your back on it, that's all.'

'I also have a life, Godfrey. I also have feelings. I've also suffered. I've had a hard time.'

He laughed shortly. 'Please. You're funny. You don't know what hardship means.'

'That isn't true. I've been through a painful divorce. All right, it's not the same sort of suffering. But you can't just push that aside. What about my son? What about Patrick? Do you know what he's been through?'

'Please. Please. That's white man's suffering you're talking about now. Patrick had a bad time when he was in the army. What was he doing in the army in the first place? He didn't have to go.'

'He *did* have to go, actually.'

'Why? Because the law says so? The law is illegal, don't you understand that? It's always a choice, Ellen. He chose to go. I don't feel sorry for him. You *chose* to get married, you *chose* to get divorced. I'm sorry about your terrible suffering, but you chose it for yourself. White people's pain. What happened to us here in this country is something different. We didn't choose it. It was forced on us.'

'I didn't force it on you,' she yelled. 'I didn't do it to you!'

'Yes, you did!' He was also shouting now, his voice inflated hoarsely with anger. 'You think you're not the same as the other whiteys now. You think you're so radical and amazing. Why? Because you're fucking a black man? Do you think you can fuck history away, Ellen? Is that what you think?'

'Don't talk like that. Don't talk like that to me.'

'Don't you try to shut me up. I'm not your *boy*, you understand me? You listen to me for a change. Let me tell you about what happened here. Let me tell you about forced removals. Let me tell you about Bantu education. About *Koevoet*, about what the army is doing on the border. Let me tell you –'

'I know about that!' she screamed.

'Oh, yes, you know. You know because you read it in the newspaper. You go to your stupid liberal meetings and you think you've changed the world. But you haven't lived these things. You don't know what it means, because of this. *This*.'

Here – she showed me afterwards – he leaned forward and pinched her hard. For the rest of the trip she carried a bruise, a tiny blue butterfly pinned to her neck. She let out a cry of pain and shock, and then he burst out of the room, slamming the door behind him. His footsteps jolted away down the stairs. For a while afterwards I couldn't move; I stayed pressed to the wall.

When I went out into the passage the fat lady called to me from downstairs. 'Is everything all right up there... ?'

'Yup,' I said. 'We're all fine.'

I went in to my mother. She was sitting on the edge of her bed, crying into a tissue. She was dressed in her underwear, her feet crossed over each other on the floor. She looked lost and somehow very young. I sat down next to her and put my arm around her shoulders; she leaned her head on me.

'Fucking bastard,' she said.

'He's upset. He'll calm down.'

'He's upset. What about me?'

'You're upset too.'

'You're right, I am. I'm very upset. This isn't going to work out, Patrick.'

'Don't you think so?'

'Let's go out for a drive,' she said. 'I have to think.'


We drove eastward, out of town. The tar went on for a while, then we came to a gravel road going off on one side. We followed it, leaving the houses quickly behind, and were engulfed again by the desert. Not much further on we came to another border post. Again, the two soldiers, guarding a wasteland of dunes. 'Don't you get lonely here?' my mother asked them.

'*Ja, mevrou,*' one said. He seemed a bit startled at the question, or perhaps it was at my mother's tear-swollen face. 'Where are you going? To the Moon Landscape?'

'Yes,' she said. 'That's exactly where we're going.'

As we drove on, I said, 'What is it, this moon landscape?'

'I don't know, but it sounds right for this afternoon.' She fished out her tissue again. 'Oh, Patrick,' she said, 'men are such bastards.'

'I know. I don't like them much either.'

'Well, we don't have to worry about them now. We're going to the moon.'

Half an hour later, we came to a blue-grey terrain of gorges and peaks, spilling away as far as the eye could see. There was a hissing of wind as we got out of the car and started down into the foothills. Underneath that thin sound, the silence was immense, and neither of us felt like talking. As if by mutual consent we wandered away from each other. I followed a canyon of crumbling black stone and in two minutes I was utterly alone. I sat down for a while on a rock. In the blasted emptiness, little threads of life followed their course. I saw a tiny cactus, wearing a single yellow flower like a cockade. At my feet, perfectly preserved, the white carapace of a beetle. I broke it under my heel.

I walked on again. I kept to the shade at the foot of the hills, but from time to time I saw my mother off in the distance, stalking along the long spine of a ridge. She liked to be high up, visible and dramatic, back-lit by the sun. At one point a tall cliff rose up where I was walking and I lost sight of her completely for a while. When the cliff dropped away, there she was, naked on the top of a nearby hill. The hill was an odd conical shape, and she had dropped her clothes in bright patches as she climbed up.

Now she was turning round and round, arms outspread, no doubt with her eyes closed. A soft pink plant, twirling its tendrils, sending signals into the stratosphere. Far up above her, like a dream she was having, a tiny jet unzipped the sky.

She saw me and yelled across, her voice indistinct: 'Hey, Patrick! Get undressed!'

I shook my head and sat down against a boulder to wait for her. After ten minutes or so, it was too hot, and the novelty had worn off, and she started to descend. The clothes went back on, item by item, and then she was on level ground, crunching her way toward me. By the time she arrived, she was fully clothed again, and hot and burnt-looking.

'You should try it,' she said crossly. 'Such absolute freedom.' She held out her hand to show a bright little graze. 'But I slipped on the way down.'

'Shame,' I said.

We started to walk back, both gone a little flat. By now we were tired and we walked without pleasure. A cold wind blew down into our faces from the direction of the road. From nowhere she suddenly asked me, 'Have you ever been in love?'

'Yes. Once. I think. I'm not sure.'

'You never told me about it.'

'I don't think I knew at the time.'

We got back to the hotel in the late afternoon, the shadows already long and turning blue. We both stood in the upstairs passage for a moment and then she went into her room and I went into mine. Everything was quiet for a while and then I heard low, abrasive sounds. I thought it was them again, starting up a new argument, but the sounds got loud and guttural, and then I realised what I was listening to.

# CHAPTER NINE

Valium comes in a variety of shapes, though it's mostly round. The colours are variable too, but I have a penchant for blue. When I first started taking it, even weak doses knocked me out; but now my immunity has grown. Fifteen grams hardly affect me.

I take Valium at least twice a day. I need them to sleep at night. They make sleeping easy, but dreamless. They take effect quickly, thinning the blood, releasing the tightly bunched muscles. The mind flattens out. 'Take these whenever you feel any anxiety,' the nurse at 2 Military Hospital told me. This was down in Cape Town, in February, almost a year after I'd left for the border. I had my own room, with a bed I never had to leave unless I wanted to. Occasionally doctors came by to see me. It was in that bed, that room, that they told me I was to be discharged.

'From the hospital?' I said, dazed.

'From the army.' The colonel was kindly; he kept squeezing my shoulder in a familiar, reassuring way. 'It's an honourable discharge, my boy. Don't look upset.'

If I looked upset, it was because the mad, sad trauma I contained was spilling over. It had all unravelled quickly in the end. I'm not sure of how one event connected to another, or even whether there was a connection. But it seemed to begin when Lappies was killed. That was in November, about a month after our midnight encounter on guard duty, which neither of us ever mentioned and which we certainly never repeated. He and five others were on patrol; I was back in camp. We heard later they'd been caught in an ambush. All six of them had been blown away and left there in the bush. This news was conveyed to us by Commandant Schutte, whose ferocious impassivity was strained to the limit. It had been a bad month. He had lost twelve men already in the past two weeks. These losses reflected badly on him, even though more men were being flown in all the time.

Afterwards I walked alone through the camp, not sure of where I was going. I felt deeply, vulnerably alone. There was a sudden, pervasive sense of unreality to everything. I remember thinking how much the camp had grown. The veld was being cleared at one point to make place for new rows of tents. There were new faces too, young faces, shiny with fear and uncertainty. I walked between the tents, the faces, as though they were very far away from me, unable to touch on my life. The sky was vibrating overhead like a white, translucent veil, concealing immanent truths behind it, on the point of revelation. But it didn't quite tear.

What followed on from that I'm not entirely sure. I have a vague memory of standing at the fence, my fingers hooked into the mesh, staring out. I'm told that I set out walking, or tried to, through the main gate, into the bush. But I don't remember that part. The next clear image that I have is of being in front of the commandant, who was staring at me with eyes as hard and lethal as rifle-barrels, and him saying to me, 'Are you well, Winter?'

'Yes, Commandant.'

'Are you feeling all right?'

'Quite all right, Commandant.' I was standing at attention in front of him and suddenly this scenario, and his exaggerated concern, seemed ridiculous. I had to stifle an urge to giggle.

'I'm glad to hear it,' he said. 'This place is for men, not girls. You're not a girl, Winter.'

'No, Commandant.' The giggle was almost at the level of my mouth now; I pressed my lips together to hold it in.

Suddenly he seemed to fix me in his mind. 'You're the one who can't play rugby,' he said at last.

'Yes, Commandant. I mean, no, Commandant.' But this damning truth was very sad to me, and killed the laughter instantly. Now I wanted to cry.

He stared at me for a long time in silence. I became lucidly aware of small details and sounds, everything around me heightened to the point of being painful. Then he seemed to resolve something in his mind and took a step closer to me. Almost whispering, he said, 'You're all right, you say.'

'Yes, Commandant.'

'Good, good. Because they need some help at the choppers over there. Loading up some bodies. And I think you're just the man to do it.'

'Yes,' I said. 'I can do that.'

But I knew already that I couldn't do it, I wasn't the man for the job. Amongst the heavy body bags, stacked up like so many groceries next to the helicopters, was the body of Lappies, my friend. It didn't help that I didn't know, couldn't see, which one was him; in some way they had all become him. So I stood in the sun, my hands slipping on the plastic, heaving the weight up and in, over and over, knowing that I couldn't do this, couldn't do this, even while I was busy doing it. Some vital part of myself was used up in the effort required simply to perform the mechanical actions and by the time I walked away afterwards, past the watching commandant, I had reached empty inside.

'Good, Winter, good.'

'Yes, Commandant.'

I stood in the shade of a thorn tree and watched the helicopters start up. The heavy rotors, which seemed so immobile, bent over as if heavily weighted, started churning and lashing, till they were blurring around in dust and screaming wind, and then the improbable metal bodies underneath them lifted up and floated. They disappeared over the fence, over the trees, their noise and fury becoming a tiny point of sound, which then blipped out into silence. Gone.

I kept going for a while after that. How many days exactly, what happened in those days, I don't know. There was the same intermittent, patchy feel to my memory, in which certain random moments are clear. I remember walking at least one patrol, feeling absurdly calm. The whispering bush, seething with air, was only part of my mind. I had that same crazy desire to laugh when I saw the tension of the other men around me, fingers clenched tightly on the triggers of their rifles.

By contrast, everyday things could fill me with terror. I could lie on my bed, reading a book, and feel the world disassemble into separate and threatening parts. In an instant everything was odd: the blankets, the pillows, the pages. I couldn't fit these things together, I couldn't make them work. It was a universe and world to which I did not belong: I wanted to run from it, bawling into the bush; but I stayed, hunched over, the palms of my hands jammed into my eyes.

Somebody called the commandant again. He was in front of me, standing next to my bed, looking down at me. When I saw him I tried to stand up, but he held up a hand. 'Don't move, Winter. Let me look at you.'

I didn't stir or speak. He seemed inordinately huge, and his shadow behind him, cast upwards against the canvas, seemed huger again. After a long time he said:

'Are you trying to be funny?'

'No, Commandant.'

'Don't fuck with me, Winter. You can't get out of here by acting.'

'I'm not acting anything, Commandant.'

He went away after a while, and then he sent the chaplain to speak to me. The chaplain was a nervous, pale man, always perspiring. He said, 'What is the matter with you, Rifleman?'

'I don't know. Is something the matter with me?'

'It seems so. Do you believe in God?'

'I don't know.'

'Have you tried to believe?'

'Yes. No. I don't know, I've never thought about it.'

'You've never thought about God?'

'Not like that, I don't think so, no.'

'Will you pray with me, Rifleman?'

'Yes, all right.' I closed my eyes while he started his intoning, but I opened them soon afterwards and watched him – his fervour, his sweaty desperation. I suspected that even if I hadn't been ill, this man and my talk with him would have seemed ridiculous to me.

Then the doctor came. He was a big, fat, bullish man, not known for his sympathetic views of national servicemen. He also sat and talked to me for a long time, hunched up in his own version of prayer. Then he went away again. I don't know what he thought about my state, or what he reported to the commandant, but nothing happened for a while after that.

My life was receding, becoming transparent and thin. It was as if the world was wearing away around me, leaving only bright, particular patches of memory. I have a vivid impression, for example, of something I saw one day, but no idea of where I saw it: a dead elephant, shot by soldiers for cruelty or fun, lying on its side, swelling with gas and maggots. Its tail had been cut off and somebody had carved their initials into its side with a pen-knife. But I cannot explain this image, any more than I can explain what else was happening to me. By this time I was losing the power of speech. I struggled to finish sentences, ordinary words disappeared in my mouth when I needed them. And none of this felt terribly important; or not to me. It bothered the people around me, however – perhaps because their lives were placed in jeopardy. One day, when I was on guard duty, I wandered off from my companion into the grass near the gate. I squatted behind the complex pattern of a thorn tree and pressed the barrel of the rifle into my mouth. That was another distinct moment: the smoky, metallic taste of imminent death, one finger-flicker away from me. But the other soldier I was with came looking for me and let out a sudden cry of alarm. I dropped the gun and stood up, grinning, as though I'd been caught doing something naughty and embarrassing.

'It was a joke,' I said. 'I was just joking.'

But he kept staring at me, his face strained and pale.

That night, maybe – or some other night completely – my mind finally tipped over. It happened slowly. I was lying on the bed, very calm and quiet, still wet from taking a shower. Other soldiers were moving around me, doing their little everyday tasks. Then time altered shape. Seconds stretched out like years; a lifetime unfolded inside me. I stood up from the bed, trying to say something, but I didn't know what, or how.

A soldier in the next bed, looking very alarmed, said, 'What? What?'

Life, I saw clearly, was pain. A white, molten stream, it poured without end, hardening into temporary form: the bodies around me, the beds, the tent, the ground, were the physical shape of this pain. But I was melting, I was breaking the mould. I felt my knees cracking. I sank to the ground. Then I started to cry. I beat with my fists on the ground.

'Winter's gone *bossies*,' somebody said.

I opened my mouth and fetched up a scream from deep inside me, from all the years of my little life behind me. Then everything caved in inside. A light went out in my mind. Around a kernel of quietness, the very core of me, I felt frenzy and motion: my limbs thrashing, my teeth grinding, my head bashing in the dust. But I was safe inside, buried out of reach.

After a space of no-time a doctor was next to me, taking my pulse, prodding my back. He tried to turn my head. 'Please,' he said. 'Please open your eyes.'

I could hear him, but he was somewhere else. I was inside my mother, suspended in space; I couldn't talk to him or gesture to him; I could only watch from a long way off.

He took my hand. 'Please give a squeeze if you can hear what I'm saying.'

I tried to do it, but the impulse shot off obliquely into the void.

Then footsteps, voices, a bag being opened. Then a sensation that wasn't a pain, which I knew was a needle in my arm. Then no more sensation.

When the world resumed its business with me, it was morning, striped through with sunlight. I was lying in a narrow white cot, with similar beds around. There were people in some of them, plugged into intravenous drips. A bandaged form lay nearby. But now I wasn't buried so deep; there was a connection between my will and my body. I heaved myself up onto my hands.

And it was only then that I sensed him. Behind me, close to my head, sitting in a chair. Watching me.

'Winter,' he said. 'You're alive.'

'Commandant.'

'At ease. Relax.' His tone was neutral. 'How are you feeling?'

'I'm all right. I don't know what happened to me.'

'You had a little freak-out.'

'I guess so.'

He smiled, but it was a dead, cold smile. His eyes didn't change. 'You're going to get better, Winter. You're going to be a soldier again and go out and kill terrorists.'

'Yes, Commandant.'

'You're not a girl. You're a man. A white South African man. We need you with us.'

'I know that, Commandant.'

'Every body lying in bed in hospital is one more body on their side, Winter. I hope you know that.'

'I do know that.'

'Some people,' he said, shaking his head in amazement, 'some people want to get out of here so badly that they do things to themselves. They hurt themselves to escape. Can you imagine that? I had a soldier once, national serviceman like you, who shot himself in the leg.'

'I'm not like that, Commandant.'

'I know that. I'm just saying. You get people who fake cracking up, just to escape their duty. But I know you're not like those people. You're a man.'

'Yes, Commandant.'

He smiled again and got up quickly to his feet. 'Have a rest, Winter,' he said. 'See you soon.'

I lay for a long time after he was gone, watching motes of dust swirling like billions of tiny planets in his wake. Then the bandaged man opposite me rolled in his bed, emitting a bubbling groan. I pulled back the sheets, put my feet on the floor. I sat, staring down at my ankles.

I was naked. Someone had undressed me; my clothes were packed neatly nearby. I felt curiously fine and happy. I decided I had to do my duty – to the commandant, to my country – and return to my tent. But as I reached for my pants, a crack opened in my head and I fell through it. As on the previous night, my body slid down to the floor, and further: into oblivion and night.

I don't remember much of that second collapse. It involved doctors again, and needles, and drugs. And then I was being carried on a stretcher to a helicopter. The heat thudded down, my body was tired and sore. But I managed to lift my head up and saw him, as I knew I would: Commandant Schutte, watching from his usual place, close to the trees. He was completely upright, very still and stiff, as he observed what was surely my triumph.

But I felt no sense of victory as the metal doors closed and the great engines started up. The machine that carried me was shaking with tremendous power, but there was no power left in me; I felt empty, hollowed out.

I was taken to hospital in Pretoria. There I was treated with brusque jollity by nurses who monitored my progress with charts and graphs. I only ever saw one doctor, who came by every morning to sit next to the bed and make furtive notes while he spoke to me.

'Can you try to describe how you feel?'

'I can't put it into words, really.'

'Try.'

'I feel far away from everything. I feel... dislocated. Not part of life.'

'Whose life?'

'Mine. Everybody's. *Life*.'

'Mmm. Go on.'

'I don't care. I don't seem to care about anything.'

'Mmmm.' He was scribbling furiously.

'That's all, really,' I said. 'That's how I am.'

My father came to see me. He sat in a chair at the head of the bed, where the psychologist also sat. My father was uneasy. He clasped his hands between his knees and shifted from buttock to buttock.

'Are you all right?' he said.

'Yup,' I replied.

'Do you want to talk about anything?'

'No. Not that I can think of.'

He looked pained. He seemed to feel that something had happened to alter me, and that he couldn't speak to me in the normal way. He sighed and cast around him and said, 'It's a nice room they've put you in.'

'No, it isn't. It's a horrible room.'

'You're right,' he said. 'It isn't a nice room at all.'

A week or two later I was sent down to 2 Military Hospital in Cape Town. My mother was acting in a play at the time, which was why, she told me, she couldn't come up to Pretoria to visit me. But now she spent every morning with me, bringing books and chocolates and tapes. She chatted without stopping, mostly about herself and her life, but the endless noise and bustle were somehow comforting to me.

It was there I was told that I'd be discharged.

It was there I was given Valium for the first time.

And it was there, on the day I was to leave, that my mother confessed about Godfrey. I had packed up my bags, and they lay on the floor. An unseasonal rain was falling outside. We were waiting for some forms to be brought to the ward, which I had to sign. My mother leaned forward, wetting her lips, her eyes shining.

'There's something I have to tell you. I was going to

wait till you were out of here, but I just can't hold it in any more.'

I looked warily at her. 'What is it?'

'I think I'm in love,' she said. 'His name is Godfrey.' Then she told me the rest and sat back expectantly, her palms pressed together.

'Right,' I said. None of it mattered very much to me.

'Well, is that all you can say? What do you think?'

I smiled and shrugged. I had nothing to say. I looked at my mother as she sat there on the bed, waiting for me to be amazed and awed by her life. At that moment a shaft of light, blued by the rain, fell on her face: like the actress she was, she turned towards it, finding her spot. Then she smiled, and the smile became a laugh: a round, silvery sound, like a coin, which fell from her throat and tinkled down onto the ground. She looked very beautiful in that moment.

'Ah, Africa,' she said.

And we sat there, silently waiting.

# CHAPTER TEN

It felt wrong to be listening to the sounds of love-making between my mother and her boyfriend, so I went downstairs to get away. I had no clear idea of where I was heading. I thought of a walk again, out to the long jetty, but when I got to the foyer the early news was on and I sat down to watch. One of the main items dealt with rumoured SWAPO incursions from the north, supposedly timed to sabotage the elections; and this was followed by a story about 'the Andrew Lovell case.'

They showed a still photograph of him, which turned out to be the same image featured on Godfrey's posters. Then they cut to an interview with the porcine police spokesman, smirking behind his moustache. 'The South West African police,' he told us smugly, 'have detained somebody in connection with this murder.' A forty-three-year-old man, an Irish national, had been taken into custody in Windhoek. The man, it was believed, belonged to an undercover white extremist group and was a former member of the IRA. He had not yet been charged, but he was 'assisting police with their investigations.' A second arrest was imminent.

The police official seemed pleased. He spoke of the 'dedication and commitment' of the security forces. 'Round-the-clock work made this possible.' Working with few clues and 'in the face of anti-South African propaganda', the results of the investigation were a 'triumph for the impartial work of the officers concerned.'

The camera showed us the face of the suspect: a square face, with close-cropped hair, military in appearance. The nose was skew, broken perhaps; the eyes were dark and blank. The photograph was a little blurry and indistinct, like the facts surrounding the man himself: who was he, why was he being offered up like this, who was he working for? In the murky waters of South African politics, it was hard to know anything.

I was caught up in the story, its various motives and outcomes, while the news had passed on to stories further afield – 'unrest in Soweto.' I wasn't listening, and it took a voice close to my ear to break my reverie. The voice said:

'He deserved it.'

I looked up. At the next table was a meaty man in khaki, in his late thirties, with a spade-shaped beard. He gave the impression of quiet power. His eyes – set wide in a flat, furrowed face – were as blue and limpid as gas.

'I don't know about you,' he said, 'but I think he deserved it.'

His accent was Afrikaans and his voice slightly hoarse. But it wasn't an ugly voice; it had a measured, calm tone.

'I don't know about you,' he said, 'but I have no time for people who turn their backs on their own kind. It's all right for blacks who want to change the system – if I was in their place, I'd want the same thing. But whites who go joining the black side... I ask you, what do they want?'

'Maybe he wanted justice,' I said. The big word – 'justice' – sounded false in my mouth.

He repeated the word, tasting its strangeness. 'Justice. Justice. Now that sounds funny to me. Justice for one man means a raw deal for someone else. Human nature, wouldn't you say?'

I looked down at my shoes.

'Or are you going to tell me,' he went on, 'that you believe in justice, peace, truth? Is that what you believe? You seem like an intelligent young man to me. Surely you know something about how the world works by now. Surely you know it's dog-eat-dog, that's the only big truth out there.'

I didn't know what to say. In some way, he sounded reasonable and worldly to me. I didn't want to come across as naïve and silly, though all the ideals he was mocking had seemed obvious and real till a moment ago.

'The name's Blaauw,' he said, 'Dirk Blaauw.' He held out a big, brown hand. 'I've seen you in the bar. I've seen you with your mother and her friend.'

'Yes,' I said. 'How did you know she's my mother?'

He tapped his head knowingly and winked. He had a sense for things, he meant; life held no big surprises for him.

'And what is your name?'

'Patrick Winter.' I shook his hand.

'Ah, now that's a name. A very English name. But with a lot of history, a lot of mystery. It sounds like the name of somebody with a *story* to tell.'

It was hard to tell if he was mocking me or not. His voice and face seemed full of earnestness and irony at once, so that both, or either, were possible.

'Who are you going to vote for,' I asked him, 'in the election?'

'I don't live here. I'm a South African, like you.'

'Where are you from?'

'West coast. Near Malmesbury. I'm a farmer.'

'My grandmother has a farm in that area too.'

'*Ja*? What is her name?' When I told him, he made an exclamation of amazement. 'Man, we are nearly neighbours. And you? Are you from the farm too?'

'We're from Cape Town,' I said carefully.

'And what are you doing in this part of the world?'

'Um, we're just here for the week. My mother has business.'

He stared at me with those blue blowtorch eyes. I felt, suddenly, as though I had told him too much – far more than I had intended to – and that an undefined danger lay concealed beneath his innocent interest. It was only later that I wondered what *his* business was there, at that particular time. But now, as if anticipating this very question, he said carelessly, 'I'm doing some farm stuff up here. But my car broke down. I've been waiting three days for them to repair it. But they have no parts. That's the future for us, Patrick – no spare parts.' He laughed loudly.

I stood up. 'I'd better go.'

'I was about to buy you a drink.'

'Not tonight,' I said. 'I've got to get some sleep.'

'Just one quick one in the bar.'

'Maybe tomorrow.'

'All right. Tomorrow. And tell your mother she's welcome to join us.'

'I'll tell her.'

I hovered for another second, unsure how to leave. He suddenly leaned forward and took hold of my wrist with a strong but soft grip. 'Listen,' he said, apparently friendly, 'I didn't mean to offend you just now.'

'How? When? I don't know what you mean.'

'Yes, you do. With what I said about... him. The man on television.'

'Oh, that. I wasn't offended.'

'I hope not. I didn't mean anything bad. I'm not a racist. I just have certain views, I see the world in a particular way. But I'm not a racist. I have no problem with your mother's friend, for example. You can invite him for a drink too, no problem.'

'I'll tell him,' I said. 'But I'm sure he won't come.'

He let go of my wrist. 'As long as you understand.'

'I understand,' I said. 'Goodbye.'

'Goodbye, Patrick Winter. Goodbye.'

In the painful, gory business of ending their marriage, my parents had done a lot of fighting. All the pent-up poisons had come to the surface and burst out. A lot of ugly things had been said, some of them true. I had lain in bed and heard them going at each other downstairs, night after night. The sound of breaking glass is forever bound up in my mind with the smashing of more delicate things.

None of this went on now with Godfrey, though this was, in its way, my mother's most significant relationship since leaving my father. But in the days that followed that loud argument, I knew that she was shedding it, or him. It was a cold leaving. Like a noble cause she'd taken on too passionately, he had begun to pall in her eyes. She wouldn't admit it at the time, but I could see it in the way she spoke to him, in the way she responded when he touched her. He wasn't an idea any more; he was too real.

Later she told me: 'It was all the rhetoric that did it. I just couldn't bear it. It tired me.'

'You said that was what you loved about him. You said he cared deeply about things.'

'He's so young.'

'You liked that too.'

'And he was so rough. In bed, you know. I need a little tenderness, I need to be *held*. It was the latent violence,' she announced, with enormous conviction. 'It frightened me.'

I didn't go on, though I could have. 'You found that attractive too,' I could have said. 'You told me you liked being treated like an object, white men were so tame and weak... '

There was no point. She changed her positions the way she changed her clothes, and she didn't care to remember how she'd felt in the past. At the time I was sorry for Godfrey. I thought he had no idea of what was coming. Now I think he did know; I think he didn't want to give her the satisfaction of being hurt.

The morning after the fight and our drive out to the Moon Landscape, I went into their room. Godfrey was downstairs, having breakfast. My mother, wrapped in a kikoi, was brushing her hair at the mirror. I sat next to her on the stool, pressed up close as we'd used to sit when I was young. But years had passed, and there was grey now in her hair, and my face wasn't smooth and empty any more.

'Tell me about Godfrey,' I said.

She hadn't expected this question. She put the brush down. 'What do you want to know?'

'Where does he come from?'

'A little town somewhere north. I forget the name.'

'When did he come to Windhoek?'

'A few years ago. He came to study. The academy gave him a scholarship, or he wouldn't have been able to afford it. His background is very poor, that I do know. His father is dead, so he brought his mother to the city with him. But you saw how they live.'

'Why did he do drama?'

'I don't know, really. I've wondered about that too. I think he meant to do it just as a filler in first year, but then he discovered he liked it.' She nudged me. 'All these *questions*.'

'And his politics? Where does he get it from – his anger... ?'

'Oh, God, I don't know. With a background like that, wouldn't you want to change things... ?' Something about this disturbed her; she picked up the brush again and began pulling it through her hair. 'Patrick, I want to get dressed. I'll see you downstairs.'

I wasn't sure myself where these questions were coming from, but I was interested in Godfrey – more interested than I'd been in any of my mother's other lovers. Maybe more interested than I'd ever been in my father. When I got downstairs he was already finished breakfast and was heading out the door. 'Where are you off to?' I said.

'For a walk on the beach. Want to come?'

I was hungry, but I went along. The sand was stained blackly with oil, but it was good to be standing at this point where three deserts converged: the land, the ocean, the sky. The noise of the waves filled up the silence, so that the lack of conversation wasn't awkward.

After a long pause, he said, 'I'd better get going. I have a lot to do.'

'What?'

'Well, the rally. The funeral service. I have to organize everything.'

'Is it a rally or a funeral service? They don't sound like the same thing.'

He gave a snorting laugh. 'In politics, it is often the same thing. Death and freedom, two sides of the struggle.'

'All right,' I said. 'Let's go back. My mother will be wondering where we are anyway.'

But we didn't move. Something kept us standing there, shoes in hand, the white water roiling and dragging round our feet. After another long silence I said to him:

'You shouldn't treat her badly. You should take care how you speak to her.'

I had meant this as good advice: a way of keeping her. But he stiffened, and I saw he'd understood me differently. He thought I was telling him what to do.

'It's part of my culture,' he said. 'Women don't answer men back.'

'It's part of your culture you should think about changing.'

He made an impatient sound with his mouth and wagged a forefinger at me. 'Always forcing us to change our culture. Always your way. Always the white way.'

I blushed. 'That wasn't what I meant. I was just trying to talk to you. Not all black people – just you.'

But he didn't seem to hear. There was a sizzle of underlying anger in his voice, perhaps the remnants of his argument with my mother. 'White people,' he said. 'You make me laugh. You're so concerned with yourselves. Your own little lives. You have no nation. Just people. You're so... '

'What? Selfish?'

'*Ja*. Introspective. Neurotic – you're neurotic. Look at you, for example. You're in love with your mother.'

I was stung and speechless for a second. Then I said, 'Well, so are you.' It was a useless reply, but it was the only one that came to me.

It turned out to be the best answer, because in a moment he started laughing. He roared and slapped his stomach. The tension between us, which was about to turn into ugliness – an ugliness, I now think, that was always somehow just below the surface between the three of us through those days – folded inside out and became something else, something innocuous and innocent. We were just two young men talking on the beach. He came closer to me and put one arm around my shoulders. 'Let's go back,' he said. 'You're right, your mother will be waiting.'

My mother said she had a headache and wanted to rest in the room. So Godfrey and I went out alone. We drove to the SWAPO office where I had sat on the kerb the morning before, watching the town come to life. We parked outside the butchery, where yesterday the pigs had been hanging in the window, and went in and up to the first floor.

The office was smallish and open plan, washed through

with light. There was a great deal of activity – people writing or talking on the telephone. They were happy to see Godfrey; there was a lot of hand-slapping and chatter. He didn't introduce me to anybody, but I was accepted as a background detail to his life that didn't need to be explained. I followed him to a back office with a telephone where he was apparently to conduct his business. Somebody brought us mugs of coffee. I sat and watched while he made a few calls, feeling both near and very far from all of this. I was, I think, a little in love by then.

Then he got up, just as abruptly as he'd sat down, and jerked his head at me to indicate that we were leaving. I scurried along in his wake, back down the stairs to the car. Some of the people from upstairs had been loading up the boot with banners and ropes and what looked like part of a podium. Now we drove out on the road I'd taken with my mother yesterday. But we didn't go far: just to the edge of the township, where the desert took over. There was a sort of natural arena, a shallow basin of sand, ringed on the far side with the first high dunes. It was obvious that this was where most communal activity in the township took place: there were improvised goalposts for soccer, and a fair amount of rubbish lying around. But it was shaping up now for the rally or service that was taking place later. There was a half-built podium, and somebody was hanging bunting around it. A loudspeaker was already in place. I could see a generator nearby and electric cables lying like random cracks in the earth.

I was a little lost here. I'd come along to help, but nobody asked me to do anything. Godfrey ignored me completely. In a minute or two he was off somewhere, helping with putting up some kind of barrier, and I was left to wander aimlessly through the little crowd. There were a lot of children and idlers from the township, come to watch what was happening, and I became one of them. It wasn't a bad role to play.

It took me a while to notice the one other white person present, a woman a bit older than me, sitting up near the crest of a dune, her knees close to her chin, arms hugging her legs. She didn't seem fascinated by the little scene unfolding below her; she seemed, if anything, to be wishing it away. I went closer to her by degrees, wandering in random loops nearer to the bottom of the dune, but if I'd hoped she'd notice me she gave no sign. Eventually I cast aside my shyness and made a direct approach, up the face of the dune. It turned out to be a long climb, the sand crunching and squeaking under my feet, and I was gasping by the time I neared the top. She still hadn't looked directly at me.

I sat down next to her. The view was surprisingly impressive, all human figures in it reduced to ciphers. I said to her, 'Are you coming tonight?'

She didn't answer. I turned my head to look at her. From close, her little triangular face was dark. She was quite pretty, with thin curved eyebrows, a long narrow nose pierced with a stud. But there was something colourless about her, a hollowness that chimed with something in me. I felt as if I knew her, though I'd never met her before. I said:

'Did you know him?'

Tonelessly, she said, 'He was my boyfriend.'

'I'm sorry.'

She nodded. 'So am I,' she said. After a moment a tear broke free from one eye and ran down her cheek, but that was the only visible reaction.

'I didn't know him,' I said, then felt stupid for saying it. There was no reason for me to be here, interrupting her grief, but I felt as if I wanted something, some answer or acknowledgement I couldn't give words to. 'But Godfrey, my mother's friend, he knew him. That's Godfrey down there.'

Now she did turn to look at me. Her eyes were greenish, but they seemed almost black. 'Please... ' she said. She meant, *please go away, please leave me alone.*

'I'm sorry,' I said again. 'I'll leave now. But I just wanted to say, I wish I was like him, I wish I was more like him.'

There were other words behind these ones, a confession straining to be made, but it couldn't come out. If I could have spoken I might have said something like this: *your lover who died was all that I'll never be. Though I strain and I beat, my efforts are muffled, my cries are eaten by silence. I have longed for a way to vent my country from me, to bawl it out of my head. Andrew Lovell was my other impossible self.* Instead I smiled thinly at her and got up and went back down the dune, staggering in the thick sand, trying not to look back.

When I got down to the bottom Godfrey was waiting for me. 'Come on,' he said. 'We'd better go back and shower.'

My mother wasn't in the room. I went downstairs, through the foyer, to look for her. It was by chance that I went into the bar; I knew, after all, that she wouldn't be there; but she was there, and she wasn't alone.

She was at the counter, a glass in hand, backlit by green light. At the moment I came in she was laughing, her head thrown back, exposing her throat – a pose of wanton abandon, so apparently free that perhaps only I could see how tightly twisted her legs were around the base of the stool. It took me a moment to move past her, but I knew already, in some prescient hollow under my heart, what I would see: the khaki clothes, the hairy whorled knees, the brown hat with a strip of leopard-skin tied around it. He touched two fingers to his temple in a mock salute and called: 'Patrick! You said you'd have a drink today!'

My mother swung around, her eyes bright with unintelligent excitement. 'Darling,' she said, 'how are you? How was your day at the office?'

'Fine,' I said. 'We were setting up for the rally.'

'You didn't tell me you'd met Mr Blaauw.'

'He can call me Dirk.'

'I forgot,' I said.

'What can I get you?'

'Nothing right now. I have to go and shower. We have to get ready.'

'I'll be along in a minute, I just have to finish this gin and tonic. I've had a wonderful day. I went to the beach. I went to the shops. Look at this little bottle I found in town.' She delved into her handbag and brought out a blue glass bottle. I remembered it immediately from the German shop, the one where all the swastikas and SS swords were. It was part of the collection of everyday objects that had been distorted by the desert. 'Isn't it amazing? Look at the shape.'

'I see it.'

She picked up something in my tone and looked at me reproachfully. 'Are you cross because I didn't come along today? You don't resent me having one day off, do you?' She looked at Dirk Blaauw and rolled her eyes. 'Children,' she said. 'I'm supposed to be here for a holiday, and they get upset if you take even one day off.'

He laughed with immoderate heartiness, as if she'd been incredibly witty.

'But we aren't here on holiday,' I said.

I'd spoken levelly, but she flinched, as if I'd shouted. 'Of course we are,' she said. 'What did you think?'

'Have a drink,' he said again.

'No, thanks. I'm going to shower.' I walked across the room to the door and turned back to look. But they'd already forgotten I was there. Their heads had drawn together again in smiling collusion above the strange blue bottle.

# CHAPTER ELEVEN

'I've never dug a grave before.'

'You'll dig a lot more in your life. Anyway, it's not a grave.'

I had blisters on my hands. I paused to wipe sweat off my forehead and lifted the spade again. Godfrey was watching me, hands on hips, like a feudal overlord. Like a white master in my own country.

He was right: it wasn't a grave; it was just a little hole in the desert. We had come a bit early to the place where the rally was being held that night so that we could make this one preparation. Andrew Lovell had been cremated, and it was his express wish that his ashes be scattered in the desert. But Godfrey had decided that half of the ashes would be interred here, at the height of the rally, as a symbolic gesture.

My mother was perched on a stone nearby. She was wearing a blue scarf, which the wind had unpicked and stretched out behind her. Her mood was heavy and preoccupied, as though she had nothing to do with the two of us and our bizarre activity in the sand.

And it was true that we felt ourselves separate to her, as though she was a figure off in the distance to one side. Godfrey and I were aware of each other in a heightened way, but it was a feeling we could not put words to. In any event, what this meant to him was different, I was sure, to the meaning it had for me. For him this was some kind of perverse political lesson he was teaching; he had given me the spade to dig with as though this whole rally was for me.

'That's enough,' he said. 'That's deep enough.'

He turned away, looking suddenly bored. A few other people were arriving now, drifting in out of the lowering gloom. The SWAPO flag was snapping on a pole nearby. I wandered off, looking for a place to leave the spade. In the end I took it back to the car.

It felt to me that I wasn't dressed for the occasion. It never had become clear whether this was a rally or a funeral, but my temperament inclined me towards the ritual around the ashes and the hole in the ground. I had tried to find dark clothing, but I wasn't prepared. I had to make do with jeans and a grey shirt. But when we'd left the hotel I saw that Godfrey had made no attempt to dress soberly. He was also wearing jeans, and a T-shirt of marching black workers under a red banner that said, NAMIBIA! ONE NATION! Now I saw that the people coming in from all directions were also dressed in bright colours that spoke of celebration rather than mourning. I had to remind myself that this country was on the verge of renewal and regeneration, and the temptation to grieve belonged more properly to where I came from.

'Oh, would you look at that sky,' my mother said. 'The colours are absolutely perfect.'

She had wandered over to me. I knew her moods well enough to sense her petulant alienation. I remembered the first few times she'd been to political rallies in South

Africa, the demented fervour with which she'd described them. All the shouting and marching and rage – it was like the lid coming off her own life. But now the intensity had gone out of it for her; she was watching it from outside; she was lonely and bored.

'Let's go up that dune,' she said, 'and watch the sun going down.'

It was the same dune that Andrew Lovell's girlfriend had been sitting on. We climbed it by the same route, a laborious slog up the front face. By the time we got to the top the sun was resting on the horizon, a ball on a flat line. Almost immediately it was disappearing, sucked down behind the world, but my mother was right: the colours it left behind were perfect. The sky was a molten mess of reds and blues and pinks. Down at the bottom of the dune the shadows were complete. But a generator roared somewhere, and floodlights stuttered into life; in a moment we were looking down into a bowl of blue light. People were pouring in now, streaming in on foot from the township nearby, but down the road a steady line of cars was approaching and parking. All of this activity and arrival felt somehow centred on that little hole I'd dug half an hour ago.

And now that we were here, so high above them – though we hadn't come here to escape – there seemed to be no reason to go down again and join them. So we sat and watched, and it was as if we were amongst them, but also apart. I saw the faces: young and old, men and women, workers and thinkers, most of them black but a few white skins too. I saw, or I thought I saw, Andrew Lovell's girlfriend, less solitary and sad than before. Music was pumping out through speakers now, and the crowd was like liquid filling up the hollow bowl of sand. The mood was festive and furious, and the floodlights cast huge, wavering shadows that amplified the smaller movement.

There was no clearly defined moment when the gathering became a meeting; at some point the music was overtaken by voices. There were speakers on the podium, addressing the crowd, and the crowd answered with its own baying voice. Call and answer: it was almost religious. From above, the individual words were not distinct; it was the charge and the feeling that came through. It was angry and vital and fervent at the same time. Then somebody came to the podium, a South African man, famous enough to be familiar even to me. He was a cleric and a preacher, as well as a revolutionary; he had spent much of his life in prison. And all the fire and rhetoric of the evening seemed to be concentrated in him. The meeting was both a funeral service and a rally now; he bridged the divide easily. His voice was clear, with a hard edge, and some of the words carried up to us. He was talking about Andrew Lovell, about the future and freedom, and somehow they were all the same thing. The crowd was listening to him, not so restive now, and the responses were more focused and unified. For the first time I wanted to be down there, part of the mass, and I got up to my feet to listen.

It was at the end of his speech that the moment came when Andrew Lovell's ashes were poured into the hole in the ground. People were densely packed around the podium, it was impossible to see anything, but I felt that little act – the putting-away in the ground, the sealing-up of the earth – as something happening to me. I thought of the deaths that had touched my life: my brother, Malcolm, my friend, Lappies. I thought of my grandfather, lying under his little cartridge of soil on the farm. Of Jonas, the man who killed pigs. I remembered the SWAPO soldier I might or might not have killed on the border. Then I found myself thinking this:

*Did I shoot Andrew Lovell?*

*Yes*, I thought, *I did it.* But also: *No, because I am him.*

I don't know the meaning of these two answers – or even, really, of the question. But that was what came to me. And it was as if there were two selves at war in me, two different people with a past and a mind that had nothing to do with mine. The fracture ran through me, through my life, down to a place where my life joined with other lives.

Godfrey was coming up the dune to join us. He was frowning and I thought he was cross that we had kept ourselves away, but when he got up to the top he smiled suddenly and came to stand between us. He put an arm around our shoulders. For a moment, then, the three of us were a family, held together by the hard warmth of his powerful arms.

It was full night by now, and the stars appeared intermittently between streamers of cloud. Down below, the service, if that was what it was, had finished, and the crowd was singing. Freedom songs, songs I didn't know, but the rhythms were stirring. Godfrey was humming along, the deep vibrations transmitting themselves from his chest, and swaying gently from side to side. For a second I saw how things could be: part of a mass, of a singing congregation, the family to which I'd never belonged... and then time fell suddenly away.

I was back in a white hospital bed, with a doctor sitting beside me. 'Try to describe how you feel,' he said.

'I feel dislocated,' I told him. 'Not part of life.'

'Whose life?'

'Mine. Everybody's. *Life*.'

And the familiar sensation started up in my belly, the shaking spread into my arms. I covered my face with my hands, but I couldn't block out what I saw.

The desert covered us all. Through the flickering bodies dancing and ululating down below, I saw the sand shining through. Under the joyous thunder of voices, I heard the thin, insidious wind. Years of war and ideology, all the laws and guns and blood: the whole huge tumult of history converged on a single point, and this was what it was for – for sand. Rocks and sand and air. Barren, omnipotent emptiness. We would all disappear, every one of us, and the only thing that would stay behind was the arid backdrop of the earth. Dry and dead and voiceless.

I started to run. I broke out of Godfrey's embrace and was half-falling, half-stumbling, down the back of the dune, into the dark. I heard my mother call my name. I couldn't stop, even if I had wanted to; the pull of gravity was too strong; and then I lost my footing. It was a long, slow, violent tumble, the world sliced into panels of blackness and sky and an intermediate zone of faces, Godfrey's and my mother's, distorted with speed and alarm. When I got to the bottom I was somehow on my feet again and running, running without aim or destination, on a trajectory into the night. I could hear my own breath heaving and sawing in my chest, and the dim cries of pursuit. It felt for an extended moment that I was weightless and free, that I could continue skimming like this across the surface of the earth for ever, without stopping.

Then a huge weight crashed into me from behind and brought me down. It was like the dune itself collapsing on me, and it took a few startled seconds for me to understand that Godfrey had tackled me. He was still on top, pinning me down, gasping with effort. But the frenzy had gone out of me. I was limp, not moving anymore. With my face pressed sideways to the sand I watched my mother come staggering up and stop. 'Oh God,' she said, 'oh, my God.' Then, an actress dying badly, she collapsed forward onto her knees. 'Take a pill,' she said. 'Why don't you just take a pill?'

# CHAPTER TWELVE

I woke up in the morning with a jolt, as if something had hit me. But the room was still and quiet, washed through with light. It was long past sunrise. I got up and dressed and went downstairs.

The dining room was empty for once, the television silent and blank in the corner. A yellow glow came through the front windows, lighting the place like a church. My mother sat at one of the tables, a foot propped up on a chair in front of her. She was carefully, laboriously, painting her toenails, her face drawn inwards with concentration. She didn't look up as I sat down nearby.

Neither of us spoke for a while. She finished the nails on that foot, and picked up her hat from the table to fan her toes. Then she smiled at me. 'I've told him,' she said.

I knew instantly what she meant. There was a certain look that came to my mother's face when she was ending a relationship. It was as much a part of her as her hair, her smile. I sat and waited for what would follow.

'Oh, Patrick. It wasn't working. It just wasn't going to work.'

I had sat through these unburdenings countless times before. I knew what she wanted of me; I was supposed to murmur in agreement, nod my head, endorse by little signs the momentous decision she'd taken. I had always played my role in the past, but something was different today. Today the familiar routine depressed me.

'He was so possessive. Demanding, you know. I just need to be on my own. Maybe I should never be involved with anybody. Maybe I should be on my own.'

And on and on. I knew it all by heart. History is written by the victor, but I wasn't listening today. Somehow the room had gone silent for me, and I was watching a picture – in a nameless hotel a woman was talking, her hands gesturing dramatically as her mouth worked, all very earnest and intense, except that she was changing feet on the chair and painting a new set of toenails a lurid green.

'I don't think you should leave him,' I said suddenly.

She broke off in mid-flow, staring at me in amazement. Now sound had entered the picture again, but her voice wasn't part of it: what I was hearing was the magnified creaking of the chair under her, the bristles of the brush on her nails.

I had never said these words to her before.

'What do you mean?' she said.

'Just that. I don't think you should do it.'

Somewhere behind us, in the kitchen, somebody broke a plate.

'Well,' she said. 'I wasn't expecting this.'

'No.'

'You don't even like him, Patrick. I can see it when you look at him.'

'That isn't true.'

'Oh, you can deny it. But I know what I know. He doesn't treat you well, he patronises you – can't you see it?'

'He's all right to me. But that isn't the point.'

Her face was hardening now. 'It's not your business anyway, Patrick. It's got nothing to do with you.'

'You were talking to me about it. I'm just telling you what I think.'

'I didn't ask to hear what you think. What do you know anyway about relationships? You know nothing about what's involved.'

'Maybe you're right. But that still isn't the point.'

'What is the point then?'

The point – although I couldn't express it that way – was that Godfrey's judgement of me was true. In some obscure way, I wasn't speaking about him, but about myself. I was convoluted, involuted, bent on myself. Like the whorls of a shell, my patterns ran inward, spiralling endlessly towards a centre that didn't exist. My individuality was isolation, my personality an absence. I didn't connect with the world. I stood outside movements and masses and words. There was too much desert in me.

And I saw something else: that my mother, by contrast, wanted desperately to belong, but her glamorous strivings were hollow. Like the gestures of an actress, everything she did fell into space. We were a perfect pair, and we belonged, really, to each other.

I said, 'I don't want him to be right about us.'

'What are you talking about?'

'There's no future for us,' I said. 'We're the past. We're finished.'

For a second a real terror passed across her face; then it was replaced by irritation. 'Look what you made me do,' she said. 'I've splashed nail polish on my foot. I don't know what the matter is with you, Patrick. Sometimes I think you're really going around the bend.'

I got up and went out into the street. A mist was blowing in from the sea, turning the light grey. Feeling as if I was floating a little above the ground, I started to walk down the street. I wasn't sure where I was going, but I followed a line of palms that took me down to an avenue near the beach. At the end a park opened out, in which children were playing noisily. I sat down on a swing and rocked myself to and fro. In a little while, I knew, I would walk back up the road to the hotel, and we would pack our bags and go, and our usual lives would resume.

At the edge of the park, sitting on a bench, an old man was looking at me. I didn't recognise him at first. Then he smiled, and the dim light caught the gold in his teeth. He raised his cane, a simple, stark gesture of greeting. Before I could stop myself, I found I had waved back at him.

# CHAPTER THIRTEEN

'This is fine,' Godfrey said.

'Here?' said my mother.

'Here is fine.'

She stopped the car. She left the engine running.

'Well,' she said. 'This is it.'

Godfrey was sitting in the back with me. For the last two hours of the journey, he hadn't moved. His pose was solid and immobile, all the more so for the big pair of dark glasses he wore.

We'd left Swakopmund after breakfast. Though we had taken the main road this time – 'better than that donkey track,' my mother said – and travelled fast the whole way, it was already afternoon. Windhoek was filled with a white haze of dust.

Today was the first day of elections. Policemen stood around on the pavements. Jeeps drove through the streets. I saw people taking photographs, people making notes. It was clear we were witnessing an event.

'Are you sure you want to get out here?' my mother said. She was feeling bad at how easily she was dropping him, and trying to make up for it now by being solicitous and concerned. 'Can't we take you back for a shower? Drop off your bags?'

'Here is fine,' he said again.

But he still didn't move. He sat, immobile, as though the car hadn't pulled over yet. But we were very stationary, at the edge of a vast, dusty square in the middle of the township. We'd come here at Godfrey's request; when we'd arrived in Windhoek, my mother had driven straight to his house. But only when the car had come to a complete halt there did he lift one hand from his lap and point ahead down the street. 'Keep going.'

'What? Where to?'

'Just keep going.'

So my mother had driven on down the road. We'd passed in silence between rows of tin shacks and shanties, till eventually this space had opened out in front of us, and at last I realised what he wanted.

We were at a polling station. In the centre of the square was a cluster of striped voting booths. UNTAG officials, screened from the sun by big umbrellas, sat at tables outside. And there were South African soldiers with rifles standing around nearby.

Godfrey wanted to vote. Before going home, before dropping off his bag, before taking a shower. He was making a statement by this action, all the more poignant given my mother's haste. The whole reason for coming up here – to watch this momentous event in the history of the country – had fallen away, and all she wanted was to get home as soon as possible.

Now we were all staring through the dusty windows at the long queue outside. It was like something alive, irreducible to single individuals, though each face told its own story. There was a numb, silently suffering patience to this plodding millipede, which stretched right around the perimeter of the square all the way to the booths in the middle. As I watched, somebody came out from behind the curtain and the next person went in. It was a long, hot wait to make a cross on a piece of paper.

'Godfrey,' my mother said. 'We can't wait for ever.'

He sighed and opened the door and put a foot out onto the road. 'Give me the keys,' he said.

Only then did she turn the ignition off. He took the keys and went around to the boot, unhurried and resentful. My mother stayed behind the wheel, fanning herself with her hat, staring with an expression of faint bemusement at this spectacle of human flesh. After a moment I got out and went to the back. He didn't need help, but I lifted one of his bags out and put it down on the ground.

'So,' he said.

'So.'

We looked at each other. Although he was expressionless, I could see he was feeling bad. He moved slowly, stiffly, as though he'd broken a bone somewhere.

'I'll be seeing you,' he said at last.

'Maybe you will,' I said, although neither of us believed it.

He managed to come up with a thin smile. 'You'll come up here to live, maybe. You'll live here in exile, till South Africa is also free.'

'There are other kinds of exile,' I told him, and only after the words were out did I realise how true they were.

Then, because there was nothing more to say, we shook hands. He squeezed very hard.

'I'm sorry,' I told him.

'There are other women,' he said.

I hadn't been referring to my mother, or not only to her, but I couldn't explain. I went back around the car. As I was about to get in he called my name. When I turned back he gestured at the scene in front of us.

'Your future,' he said.

I looked at what he had shown me. I saw again the hot, dusty square, the half kilometre of waiting people. I saw the booths in the middle, the uniformed officials, the armed soldiers nearby. In the background I saw the township, the listing walls, the poverty.

A three-legged dog limped past.

I got into the car and closed the door.

'Is he finished yet?' my mother said. 'Can we go at last?'

'We can go,' I said.

She put the car in gear and swung angrily onto the road, not looking back. But I turned my head as we reached the edge of the square. He was standing exactly where I'd left him, hands hanging heavily down at his sides. By some trick of refraction, he seemed larger than he was: an idol carved out of rock. But then he bent down to pick up his bags and became human again. He started to trudge across the square, to the very back of the queue.

We went round the corner and the whole scene disappeared behind us.

'I'm glad to see the last of *him*,' Dirk Blaauw said.

He was sitting next to my mother in the front, wearing his khaki clothes, his hat with the leopard-skin tied around it. I had been staring at his neck through the whole long drive from Swakopmund: a thick, bull neck, muscled and brown. He had a small wart near his collar.

As Godfrey and I carried our bags out to the car that morning, we had seen Dirk Blaauw and my mother talking on the pavement. They were laughing at something he'd said, but they went suddenly quiet when they saw us. Then they came strolling over with studied casualness.

'Mr Blaauw's coming as far as Malmesbury with us,' my mother said. She avoided my eyes. 'His car's broken down and he's tired of waiting.'

'Call me Dirk,' he said, holding out his hand. Godfrey shook it, but he didn't say anything in reply.

When we put our bags into the boot, we saw that his luggage was already in there. He had three bulging, fat bags, taking up most of the space. He seemed concerned when he saw us struggling. 'Can you fit it all in?' he rumbled. 'Or have I squeezed you out?'

'I think we'll find a way,' I said.

For the first couple of hours he tried to get Godfrey to speak. It was almost an obsessive point of principle with him, as if he were trying to prove something. The questions kept coming aggressively: 'How do you like living here? What's the future of the country? What if SWAPO doesn't get in?' Godfrey gave terse little replies, a word or two at the most. It was as much a principle with him not to answer. Through all of this my mother and I kept silent, while I stared at the wart on that neck.

Eventually Dirk Blaauw seemed to give up. He turned his attention to my mother and the two of them kept up a flow of light chatter, making jokes and laughing. A web of white words passed between them.

Now he was shaking his head at the memory of

Godfrey. 'I'm not a racist,' he said. 'In my book, black and white are the same. But some people are kaffirs. And that was a kaffir back there.'

My mother didn't answer, but I saw her hands tighten on the wheel.

We drove south out of Windhoek, down the centre of the country. All around us, South West Africa was turning into Namibia. The air was shimmering and bright, as if a gigantic energy had been unleashed somewhere. The people we passed at the side of the road were full of jubilant animation, even in the heat. There was dancing and singing. A stooped old woman, sitting on a rock, waved a small flag on a stick. A thin, very tall young man was shouting and pushing his fist into the air. Three little schoolgirls, dressed in identical black and white uniforms, ran along next to the car, shrieking and yelling in a silly abandon, whirling their satchels around their heads.

Towards nightfall we stopped for a meal at a roadside hotel. We sat at a low wooden table in the shade. To the sad German woman who was taking our order, my mother said:

'I'll have a steak.'

When the woman was gone I turned to my mother. 'I thought you were vegetarian.'

'I need the protein,' she said. 'I have a craving for protein.'

'You're doing the right thing,' Dirk Blaauw said. 'We weren't meant to eat vegetables. Man is a hunter by instinct. A killer. The world is a jungle. Nè, Patrick?' He punched my shoulder and laughed. 'I have animals on my farm,' he went on. 'Cows, sheep, goats. And pigs. I have pigs. You must come up and visit my farm.'

'We'd love to,' my mother said. 'Patrick?'

'Yes,' I said.

'Instead of driving through tonight,' he said, 'why don't you stay over? What's the hurry? Have a good sleep, I'll give you breakfast in the morning... Stay over with me tonight.'

'All right,' said my mother. 'Thank you. All right.' To me she added: 'That all right, Patrick?'

'Yup,' I said.

Later, while we were eating, he got up and went to the bathroom. She leaned toward me. 'His eyes are amazing,' she said. 'So blue. I'm falling in love with his eyes.' She giggled.

'I think,' I said slowly, 'I think I might move out of home.'

'What?'

'It might be a good idea for me to live on my own. To get a flat by myself.'

She looked at me, then she looked away. 'You can't do a thing on your own.'

'Yes, I can.'

'Well,' she said with strangulated gaiety. 'If you think you'd like that. We'll talk about it another time.'

When Dirk Blaauw came back, my mother smiled at him. Her steak was underdone and she had a thin line of blood on her teeth.

'Shall we go?' she said brightly.

We came to the border at sunset. As we filled out the forms and had the passports stamped, one of the soldiers set his dog on the car. It was an Alsatian, with pale yellow eyes. It snarled savagely at us through the glass.

The soldier laughed at our fright. 'No problem,' he said. '*Moenie* worry *nie.*'

On the far side of the river we drove back into South Africa. We had crossed a line on a map and were in a different land altogether. Hills of grey stone loomed around us, the sky was thorny with stars.

Dirk Blaauw made a fist with one hand and struck it hard against his ribs. 'I love this country,' he said. His hoarse voice was fierce.

'Me too,' cried my mother. 'I also love it. Me too.'

They looked at each other and smiled.

'You're not tired of driving?' he said.

'No, not yet. Just keep talking to me and I'll stay awake.'

'I'm going to,' he said. 'I'm going to keep talking. Do you mind if I smoke my pipe?'

'As long as I can have a cigarette.'

He took it out of her bag for her. He slid it into her mouth. Then he pushed in the lighter in the dashboard. While they waited for it to heat up, he said to her: 'I think you're going to like my farm.'

'I have a feeling I will too.'

The lighter popped out. He held it for her, while she inclined her head. The cigarette flared and for a second their two profiles were silhouetted in this tiny red explosion. Then they both looked ahead. The car was dark again. In front of us, empty and cold, the road travelled on towards home.

## Acknowledgements

Thanks to Geraldine and Richard Aron, Gavin Lief, Kelvan and Alison Schewitz, and to my agent Tony Peake for assistance rendered during the writing of the book.

# The Quarry

When a man of the cloth gives up his body, soul and identity to another, who is watching?

On a lonely stretch of road a chance encounter leads to murder. The victim is a religious minister on his way to a new post in a nearby town and the killer decides to steal the dead man's identity in order to conceal the crime. But one of his first duties as the new minister is to bury a body that has just been discovered in suspicious circumstances. As the corpse is laid to rest the manhunt begins...

'There are thrilling images here, powerful themes and almost scarily precise writing... Galgut is at the leading edge of what is turning out to be a brilliant documentation of South Africa's post-apartheid transition.' Patrick Ness, *Daily Telegraph*

'An uncompromising journey into the heart of South Africa's darkness, written in prose that is at once stark and striking... An impressive work.' Michael Arditti, *Literary Review*

'An extremely atmospheric book in a hazy, raw and entirely realistic sense... A compelling read about guilt and evasion of truth.' Tom Hiney, *Spectator*

Atlantic Books
Paperback Fiction
ISBN 1 84354 295 1

Also by Damon Galgut

# The Good Doctor

Shortlisted for the Man Booker Prize,
the Commonwealth Writers Prize and the
International IMPAC Dublin Literary Award

Laurence Waters arrives at his rural hospital posting full of
optimism. Frank, the disgruntled deputy, is forced to share
his room with the new arrival but is determined to stay out
of Laurence's ambitious schemes. When the dilapidated
hospital is looted, the two men find themselves uneasy
allies in a world where the past is demanding restitution
from the present.

'A lovely, lethal, disturbing novel.' Christopher Hope,
*Guardian*

'Beautifully written, evoking mood and tension in precise
and exhilarating storytelling.' Joan Bakewell,
*Observer* Books of the Year

'Compulsive reading.' Clare Morrall, *Guardian* Books
of the Year

'*The Good Doctor* will be seen as one of the great literary
triumphs of South Africa's transition… by a novelist
of great and growing power.' Rian Malan, author of
*My Traitor's Heart*

Atlantic Books
Paperback Fiction
ISBN 1 84354 202 1

# Small Circle of Beings

The family – that small circle of beings where love should flourish – can also be an arid and alienating territory where hatred and violence may ignite.

*Small Circle of Beings* is set in a house far out of town, at the end of a dust road that rises up into the mountains. The desperate bondage of family life is revealed to a mother as she sits at her son's bedside where he lies sick, perhaps dying. Galgut's understated prose unpicks the emotional paradoxes of domesticity with a surprising, surreal twist. In a world where some of the most intimate relationships are those between strangers, *Small Circle of Beings* describes how children must learn to pull away from their parents if they are to find their own way.

'Damon Galgut is a writer of immense clarity and control. His prose feels as if it's been fired through a crucible, burning away all the comfortable excess until only a hard concentrated purity remains… scarily precise writing.' *Daily Telegraph*

'Astonishingly mature, subtle and understated… a remarkable collection.' *Sunday Express*

Atlantic Books
Paperback Fiction
ISBN 1 84354 461 X